HANDSOME SENTIENT FOOD POUNDS MY BUTT AND TURNS ME GAY

Eight Tales Of Hot Food And Beverage Love

CHUCK TINGLE

Copyright © 2016 Chuck Tingle

All rights reserved.

ISBN: 1530213274
ISBN-13: 978-1530213276

CONTENTS

1	Creamed In The Butt By My Handsome Living Corn	1
2	Glazed By The Gay Living Donuts	12
3	Slammed Up The Butt By My Hot Coffee Boss	23
4	Oppressed In The Butt By My Inclusive Holiday Coffee Cups	35
5	Turned Gay By The Living Alpha Diner	48
6	Bigfoot Sommelier Butt Tasting	59
7	Slammed In The Butt By The Living Leftover Chocolate Chip Cookies From My Kitchen Cabinet	71
8	Shared By The Chocolate Milk Cowboys	84
9	*Bonus Recipes*	95

CREAMED IN THE BUTT BY MY HANDSOME LIVING CORN

It's rare that you think of a down-home, Southern farmer in a suit and a tie, but I'm not your average farmer. Of course, there's nothing wrong with working the fields in a dirty old T-shirt and a straw hat, wiping the sweat from your brow as you till the brown soil. I can honestly say that I've put in more than enough hours doing just that.

But there are many different facets of agriculture, and as the work changes in this modern day and age, the men and women who make up our American farming industry are changing with it.

When I was younger, all that I really needed to worry about was rotating the crops and following the weather patterns, but these days it seems like every political issue under the sun has worked its way into the process of growing food.

The particular weekend's activity; crop lobbying.

While there was once a time that the veggies I planted were based on whatever I felt like growing, many large-scale farmers like me are currently being accosted by various companies who want their seeds sown.

I'll be the first to admit, getting wined and dined like this is quite the treat for a humble guy like me, and I've honestly started to really enjoy these conferences. It's just hard to look back and recognize that this is what the life of a farmer has become. I don't think I'll ever truly feel comfortable with my shirt buttoned all the way to the top and this tie wrapped around me like a noose.

"Excuse me," comes a deep, soulful voice, suddenly breaking my concentration.

I look up, my reminiscence of the good old days dissipating quickly as it's replaced by the smiling face of a large cob of corn.

"I think I'm over there," the striking corn says, pointing to the airplane seat next to me.

I should stand up and let him through, making the whole boarding process as quick and efficient as possible, but instead I just sit here and stare at him, completely taken aback by the vegetable's shockingly good looks.

"Are you alright?" the corn asks, snapping me out of it for a second time.

'Oh, yeah, sorry about that," I stammer, standing up from my seat and then stepping out into the aisle of our bustling jet as we prepare for take off. I wave my hand across the row of chairs, motioning the corn inward.

Even now, I can't take my eyes off of this muscular agricultural staple as he moves past me and then finally collapses into the window seat. He is perfectly toned from head to toe, a beautiful yellow glow shimmering off every kernel of his body.

When I take my seat once again, the vegetable introduces himself. "I'm Liplon," the corn tells me, shaking my hand.

"Matthew McConneymay," I reply, giving him a firm shake and trying my best to collect my sense. "I'm guessing you're flying to the agriculture conference, too?"

"What gave me away?" the cob of corn says with a wink.

I laugh, instantly charmed by the handsome vegetable. I can see why this corn in particular would be sent in to convince farmers of using his species in their fields; he has an overwhelming amount of charisma to go with his dashing good looks.

"You a corn man?" Matthew asks, cutting right to the chase.

I chuckle, suddenly feeling quite uncomfortable. "No, I can't say that I am."

"What are you growing?" the corn continues. "If you don't mind me asking, of course."

"Oh no, it's fine," I gush, waving his cares away as I try my best to remain as endearing as possible to the veggie. "Beets."

"Hmm," is all that Matthew says, smiling to himself, and then immediately turns to look out the window in silence.

HANDSOME SENTIENT FOOD POUNDS MY BUTT AND TURNS ME GAY

I have to admit, this was not the response that I was expecting from a smooth talker such as this. I had been bracing myself for the hard sell, and when it doesn't happen I immediately find myself strangely disappointed.

At first I'm not sure if I should say anything, well aware that any more conversation on the matter could spark a heated debate and a sales pitch that I would, unfortunately, be forced to decline. My curiosity has gotten the best of me, though, and regardless of whether or not the corn is currently playing me like a fiddle, I need to know more.

"What?" I finally ask.

Liplon glances back at me. "I'm sorry?"

"What does hmm mean? Why should I be growing corn?"

Liplon smiles. "I mean, when's the last time you sat down and bit into a nice, juicy piece of corn? Like, really enjoyed it in a situation where your focus was entirely on the cob itself. Maybe with some salt and butter? I don't know, whatever floats your boat."

I shrug, suddenly realizing that I truly don't remember the last time this had occurred. Lately, it's been all beets at the house and, although they can certainly hit the spot of you know what you're doing, the thought of a piping hot corn on the cob really does sound fantastic at the moment.

Liplon can see the expression on my face and just laughs knowingly to himself. "See?"

"I just don't know if it makes business sense," I tell him.

The corn nods. "Yeah, I guess you're probably right."

Once more the handsome, muscular cob turns away and leaves me to simmer in my own thoughts.

The rest of the plane ride we don't say another word, each of us prepping for the long weekend of meetings and fancy business dinners ahead. Despite being the representative of such a massive food staple, the living corn next to me seems incredibly calm, as if he knows something that the rest of the world doesn't.

When we finally touch down in California and begin collecting our bags from the overhead compartment, the corn steps towards me and hands me his business card in one cool, calculated motion.

I take his card and read it aloud. "Corn."

"If you change your mind about your crops, give me a call," Liplon explains. "We'll do dinner."

"Sounds good," I confirm with a nod, but before I can look up to face him again, the vegetable is gone.

The first day of the conference is quite productive, a slew of meetings with several very persuasive foods who are glad to pay for my drinks regardless of the fact that I'm clearly not interested in switching crops any time soon. My main source of income is beets, however, and they always do a great job of showing my why this is a good relationship to maintain, taking me out for an incredible steak dinner in one of the fanciest restaurants I've ever had the good fortune to dine in. As a country boy, this is more than enough to keep me satisfied with the way things are going back home.

Still, there is something that continues to gnaw away in the back of my mind, a strange ache that throbs deep down in the darkest, gayest parts of my subconscious. What if I had a relationship with corn? My life is wonderful now, and I respect the hell out of beets, but could it be even better?

When we finish up our dinner my purple companions offer to pay for a taxi back to the hotel, but I decline, opting instead to clear my head with a nice long walk in the warm night air. The beets insist, but I'm steadfast in my decision and finally we part ways with a smile and a handshake.

It's not a far walk between our restaurant and the convention center, which is directly across from the hotel that I've been generously put up in. I'm taking my time, though, strolling leisurely as my thoughts drift this way and that.

No matter what I do, I can't stop thinking about the way the light had glistened off of the corn's beautiful rounded kernels, or even the succulent yet subtle taste that his body would create in my mouth. Suddenly, I find myself with the beginnings of a completely unexpected erection, my hardened member pushing gently against the fabric of my pants.

A farmer my entire life, this is the first time I've ever developed feelings for a food of any kind, let alone a vegetable. While the concept is a bit intimidating at first, it's actually quite comforting the longer I think about it. What would be so wrong for a farmer and his vegetable to take their relationship to the next level?

Nothing, I suddenly realize.

I reach into my pocket and pull out the card that Liplon gave me, flipping it over in my hand as my eyes scan the elegantly designed surface.

HANDSOME SENTIENT FOOD POUNDS MY BUTT AND TURNS ME GAY

There is a phone number on the back and, seized by a moment of erotic compulsion, I call it.

I hold the phone to my ear, listening as it rings once, twice, three times. Finally, someone on the other end picks up.

"Hello?" comes the deep voice of the handsome veggie.

"Is this Liplon? The corn?" I question.

"Speaking."

It suddenly occurs to me that I have no idea what to say, no real reason for calling other than the fact that my own sexual attraction compelled me to. The silence between us is deafening, my heart kicking into double time as my brain frantically searches for something to say.

"I met you on the plane," I finally stammer.

Liplon takes his time with this information, completely chilled as he gives this space in our conversation weight.

"Matthew, right?" the corn asks.

"Yeah, that's me," I tell him, sweet relief washing over my body as Liplon remembers my name. I'd be lying if I said that I wasn't incredibly flattered.

"You thinking about switching to corn?" the golden food asks.

"I don't know," I sigh.

"Let's meet up for a drink and talk about it," Liplon offers, "where are you at?"

I glance around, finding the nearest cross street and then describing my whereabouts to the living food.

"I'll be there in two minutes," Liplon tells me, then hangs up without another word.

I'm trembling with anticipation now, fully realizing that the consequences of breaking my current beet contracts could be utterly devastating. Depending on how angry the beets got, I could lose my farm.

Of course, that's only if I break the contract, and I suddenly realize that I've done nothing so far that could get me in trouble. For the rest of the night, I'll just keep things civil. A casual drink is nothing out of the ordinary at a conference like this.

Suddenly, a beautiful yellow convertible pulls up next to me, the top down and Liplon sitting proudly in the driver's seat. He flashes a brilliant smile.

"Get in," the handsome corn on the cob commands.

I do as I'm told and before I know it the two of us have taken off into the night, the wind whipping across my face as the city lights pass us by. Without a word between us I've found myself completely swept away by Liplon's presence, the handsome corn completely in control while I'm just along for the ride.

Soon we leave the congestion of the city behind and start cruising up the nearby hillside, winding back and forth as trees and shrubs begin to sprout up across the landscape. Our only light now is the glowing headlamps ahead and the soft wash of the brilliant full moon that hangs above.

The car begins to slow as we reach the top of a large crest, pulling off onto the side of the road in what I soon realize is a wide open lookout. The view is absolutely breathtaking, sweeping out over the entire city below, a blanket of twinkling lights.

Lipton throws the convertible into park but keeps the radio going, a soft, soothing wave of jazz pouring out from the speakers.

"Is this where you take all of your meetings?" I ask, skeptically.

Liplon shrugs. "Just the important ones."

"And what's so important about me?" I question.

Liplon thinks about this for a moment but doesn't answer, instead pushing the conversation off towards a different path entirely. "Do you see all of those lights out there across the city? Those lights are homes, and in each of those homes there is an average of four people living. Do you know how many meals that is?"

"Four people, eating three meals a day," I say, thinking out loud.

"Twelve meals a day total," the corn tells me. "Do you know how many of those meals include beets?"

"I don't know," I admit, "I never really thought about it."

"None," Liplon says bluntly. "The average person eats three beets a year, do you realize that?"

I shake my head. "Where are you getting this information from?"

Immediately, the corn reaches over and pushes a button to unlock the glove compartment in front of me. There is a quick snap as the latch comes undone and falls open, spilling a cascade of paperwork everywhere.

As my eyes pass over the swarm of text-covered pages, I begin to pick out an assortment of information; names and addresses, charts and graphs.

"What is all of this?" I question.

"After meeting you on the plane I took the liberty of doing some research on your crop selection," explains Liplon. "Your whole setup in screwed."

While I appreciate the effort that this corn has put in, I can't help but feel greatly disappointed by the way that this has gone. It was the calm and casual nature of the vegetable that had been so attractive to me, the fact that he didn't actually *push* to sell me on anything. Now, the trap has been sprung, and it's becoming achingly clearly that this whole thing is much more about business than pleasure.

"I think you should take me home," I finally sigh, gazing straight forward through the windshield.

Liplon is silent, and I can't help glancing over to see the look of disappointment and heartbreak sweep across his face.

"I'm sorry," I tell him, "this was a bad idea."

The corn starts his car and throws it in reverse, but before he can pull out I reach over and put my hand on his as it rests over the gear shift. The two of us freeze, not quite sure what to do with ourselves.

"Wait," I finally say, causing the vegetable to turn off the car once again.

Without another word I open the door and climb out, beckoning the corn to follow as I make my way down to the edge of the nearby cliff.

The view is incredible.

I take a seat and stare out across the beautiful moonlight vista, breathing in deeply from the fresh night air. Moment's later, Liplon sits down next to me.

"I have to be honest," I finally tell him, "I thought there might have been something else going on between us."

"What do you mean?" the corn asks.

"I don't know," I laugh, shaking my head, "it was stupid."

"No, what was it," Liplon insists, placing his yellow hand on my leg.

I glance over at him, suddenly feeling that same electricity that had been present before. "I guess maybe I had a crush on you," I finally admit. "When you were taking me up here, I didn't know you were just trying to get me to switch my crops. It was ridiculous of me to think that this was anything other than a business transaction."

"Oh god, it's so much more than that," Liplon suddenly blurts, leaning in and kissing me passionately on the mouth.

All of the pent up desire that has been waiting so patiently within me suddenly explodes across my body, consumed by a frantic desire to become one with this handsome corn. Even though I am completely straight and Liplon is a male, there is no denying the energy that exchanges between us any longer.

"Whoa," I gush as we pull back from one another.

"The business can wait," Lipton tells me with a smile.

"How about some corn holing?" I offer mischievously.

Without hesitation, I turn and push the giant corn back onto the grass behind us, noticing now that an absolutely massive yellow erection has started to sprout out from his ripped body. It grows larger and larger as I begin to passionately kiss my way down his kernelled chest, drifting lower with every touch of my lips until finally my mouth is hovering directly above his swollen member.

Liplon lets out a long, powerful moan as I wrap my lips tightly around his cock. I immediately get to work moving my head up and down his length, slowly and sensually at first and then building speed. Soon enough I am bobbing my head across his length at a steady pace, allowing the corn to place his hands against the back of my skull and guide me.

"Oh fuck that feels so good, Matthew McConneymay," Liplon groans, pumping his hips back against my face.

I reach down and begin to play with his hanging yellow balls, which cases the vegetable to extenuate his pumps even more.

Finally, when I feel like things have reached an erotic peak between us, I push down as far as I can to consume his rod entirely in a expertly performed deep throat.

At least, that's what the plan was. However, things don't exactly work out that way that I expected. Greatly underestimating Liplon's size, I immediately begin to choke when his dick pushes against my gag reflex. The next thing I know I'm pulling back, releasing his shaft from my depths and retching loudly.

"You're so fucking big," I admit, struggling to regain my composure. "One more try."

I gather myself as much as possible and then attempt once more, taking the corn's dick between my lips and then slowly, confidently, lowering my head onto him. This time I am much more relaxed, and when the head of his cock reaches my gag reflex I somehow allow it to pass by without any hesitation.

Suddenly, I find myself with Liplon's giant corn dick fully inserted within my throat, his balls pressed hard against my chin.

The massive food clearly enjoys being fully consumed like this, and lets me know by throwing his head back and letting out a loud, passionate sigh of pleasure.

Within the warm confines my mouth I run my tongue across his length, up and down the shaft as I slowly begin to run out of air. This continues until, finally, I just can't take it any longer and come up sputtering and choking. A long strand of saliva hangs between the corn's dick and my hungry mouth.

"I want you to pound me," I tell him, climbing up onto the vegetable as he lies sprawled out in the grass.

I'm facing Liplon as I grab ahold of his wet, slobbery dick, placing it at the entrance of my tight asshole and then carefully lowering myself onto his giant rod.

"Oh fuck, oh fuck, oh fuck," I begin to murmer, struggling to allow my body acceptance of his enormous size. For now, the corn is simply teasing my rim, pressing playfully against the edge of my sphincter until finally it opens up in one quick movement and I drop down onto him.

"Cornholed at last!" Liplon shouts gleefully as his dick impales me.

I lean forward and grip tight onto the food's shoulders, my body still desperately trying to adjust to his girth. Every ounce of my being feels stretched tight, ready to snap at any moment under the pressure of his substantial thickness.

Instead, however, the pain and discomfort that surges through me begins to subside, replaced with a strange, aching pleasure that builds and builds with every slow grind of my hips. Eventually, my movements start to speed up, turning into full on swoops of passion against the muscular corn. By now the tightness of my ass has given way completely in a wave of utter bliss, the mystical power of an impending prostate orgasm blossoming within me to replace it.

The sensation starts low and deeps, somewhere within my belly before expanding out in a series of beautiful surges. With each pump of my body across his giant rod the feeling grows, moving down my arms and legs as I tremble excitedly.

I reach down and grab ahold of my dick, pumping my hand across my length in time with my movements of the corn's meaty cock up my rump.

"I'm so close," I yell. "Oh god, I'm gonna fucking blow my load!"

Suddenly, Liplon lifts me up off of him with his muscular arms, cutting short the waves of orgasm that had been building up within.

"What was that?" I groan. "I was gonna come."

"Not yet you aren't," laughs Liplon. "The key to every business transaction is making sure that both sides are happy, we're cumming together."

"Alright," I say with a playful grin, "you're on."

Suddenly, Liplon is flipping me over on the grass so that I'm now on my hands and knees, facing out towards the seemingly endless lights of the city below. The sight may be breathtaking, but it's not until the giant corn pushes his cock deep into my asshole from behind that I literally gasp out loud.

"Fucking hell!" I cry, my fingers gripping the grass before me as Liplon gets to work from behind.

The next thing I know, the handsome corn is pounding my butthole with everything that he's got, railing me with a ferocity unlike anything that I have ever seen. It feels incredible to be dominated by him, to know that he is much stronger and more powerful than me as he uses my ass for his burning vegetable pleasure.

It's not long before the familiar orgasmic sensations begin to bubble up within me once again, spilling out through my veins like simmering erotic venom. I'm quaking hard, every muscle in my body pulled tight and then breaking like waves.

"Harder!" I scream. "Pound my ass harder, corn!"

The vegetable does as he's told, never letting up for a second as he reams my depths with a sexual prowess that makes my toes curl.

I'm just about ready to cum when the food behind me slams forward with a powerful, final thrust, crying out with a howl that echoes around us for miles. The sound is immediately joined by a spastic crackle, a series of loud pops that rattle off in rapid succession.

I look back over my shoulder in shock to discover that Liplon is erupting in a fit of passion, the kernels across his body exploding into puffs of popcorn and then shooting off in every direction.

"I'm cumming!" I corn shouts.

Within me, I can feel the strangely pleasant snap of his cock popping as well, his orgasm displaying itself in a carnal preparation of snack food. He's filling me up with his seed, pumping load after load within me until finally there's just not enough room in my ass and the popcorn comes spilling out over the edges of my sphincter, scattering across the ground below like an overfilled popcorn machine at the local movie theatre.

"There's so much corn in my asshole!" I shriek, beating myself off with an untamed fury.

Suddenly, I'm cumming as well, my eyes rolling back into my head as a massive load of jizz erupts from the end of my swollen shaft. It splatters across the ground below me, mixing with the popcorn to form a warm pearly seasoning of gayness.

When I glance back over my shoulder once more I find myself alone on the cliff side, heaps of popcorn strewn everywhere but my handsome companion nowhere to be found. A strong wind blows and scatters the food, some of it whipping off into the air and swirling away into the distance.

In this moment, I realize that Liplon is truly gone.

I look up at the crowd before me, watching as the tears stream down their faces. I realize now that I too am crying, reminiscing of my night long ago with this agricultural lover.

"That's how I met Liplon," I say, reading the final words of his eulogy aloud, "when I met him at that conference I had no idea that this breathtaking living corn would change my heart, and my butthole, forever. He will be greatly missed."

I finish and then step back from the podium as a bugle begins to play, its bittersweet song soaring out across the grass of the cemetery. To my left, the coffin full of popcorn begins to lower slowly into the ground.

"I love you," I say under my breath, unable to take my eyes off of the oblong box until it is completely below the dirt. "I'll see you on the other side, and I'm ready for some corn hole."

GLAZED BY THE GAY LIVING DONUTS

Our vacation to Southern California hadn't been a total bust, but it wasn't everything I'd hoped for either. When the guys and I loaded into Jordan's vintage convertible and hit the road from Ohio on a straight shot towards the west coast, we had big dreams; meet some cute boys, make new friends, have a few stories to share when we returned home.

And sure, we kinda did all those things, but it wasn't like the movies. Most of our time was spent sitting for days behind the wheel, and while road tripping is certainly an all American pastime, the stretches of empty nothingness along the way really start to get to you. Your friends become annoying and you stop caring about where the boys are because you're more worried about where the next rest stop is.

Salvation finally came when we cruised into San Diego on a warm summer day and found ourselves face to face with the crowded beach coastline.

The three of us parked and got out, looking up and down the miles of sand in either direction. There were beautiful people everywhere; lying out on blankets, sleeping until umbrellas. Surfers cut their way through the water like tiny dots of black against the flickering jewels of sunlight that dance and play on the tips of blue waves. It was a real life miracle, an oasis in the desert of endless gray highway between here and home.

But like everything else in life, we got used to it.

It's three days later and we are still laying out on the beach, wondering why our trip wasn't coming together like a movie montage with some fun, beachy rock song playing loudly over the top of it. The truth is, where you

HANDSOME SENTIENT FOOD POUNDS MY BUTT AND TURNS ME GAY

are doesn't change who you are on the inside, and our group is coming face to face with the fact that, deep down, we might just be really boring gay men.

"Do you ever feel trapped?" I ask out loud, lying on my back as the sun kisses my already tan skin. Jordan and Sam are on either side of me, and both guys seem to answer without words. We don't need to say it, because we are all thinking exactly the same thing.

"So how do you change it?" I add, a follow-up to my already unanswered question.

More silence as the waves rumble softly against the shore and a lone seagull calls in the sky.

Finally, Jordan speaks up. "We need adventure."

I can't help but laugh, a smile crossing my lips beneath my jet-black sunglasses. "Then what do you call this?"

"I don't know." He says.

"Maybe adventure comes from the inside." I offer. "Not where you are, but what you do when you get there."

"I'm pretty happy with my tan." Sam adds.

I laugh again. "Okay, sure. Me too. But we are heading back home tomorrow and we've got nothing to show for it."

"My tan." Sam repeats.

"A tan is only skin deep." I tell him, wisely. Now all three of us laugh.

"I wanted to have some stories, you know?" I explain. "We just graduated high-school and up until now have never really left Ohio. We're all going to college in state. It's like we're adults now but we still haven't really lived."

"Well what the fuck do you propose we do about it?" Sam asks.

"I don't know. Go out tonight?" I tell him. "Like go to one of those secret donut clubs or something?"

Being from the Midwest, the donut clubs where something of a mystery to us all, a vague rumor that found its way to us through various online forums or via hushed whispers at the local gar bar back home. We had heard tales about the utterly depraved donut scene in San Diego, but deep down I had always considered the idea of living, talking, gay pastries to be a purely European thing. Despite being invented in America, the living donuts themselves eventually started to migrate over seas in an attempt to find a more sexually liberal lifestyle, and the ones that stayed behind were eventually forced out whether they wanted to leave or not.

There was hedonism in the streets. Once the promiscuous nature of these living baked goods was completely exposed, human/donut fucking was entirely outlawed; gay, straight, all of it. The ruling led to a whole slew of human rights arguments, but despite the fact that living donuts could talk, think, and even love, they were still not considered to be legally human and therefore not afforded the same basic privileges.

Jordan rolls over on the blanket and faces me, propping himself up on his arm. "First of all, there are no gay donuts here in the United States, thanks to the Pastry Fucking Act of two thousand sixteen."

"Sure, not out floating around in public, but they're still here." I offer. "You just need to find the right donut shop."

I sit up and look to my left. Far, far down the beach where the stores become stranger and sometimes less than legal.

"They sell weed down there like it's nothing." I say. "I bet we can get a read on a hot gay donut bar."

Its not long before we find a local coffee shop with a mysterious round symbol stuck inconspicuously on the outer window, a signal to those of us who know what to look for.

Our group heads inside, trying to act as casual as possible.

The man helping us is young and fun, a surfer dude who's surprisingly handsome for being covered in tattoos with more piercing than I can count. His shop is only a small walk up the main drag of souvenir stands and bong boutiques that line the graffiti covered beach boardwalk.

"What would you like?" The handsome young guy asks. "The dark roast is fresh!"

"Actually, I'm not really in the mood for coffee." I tell him, my heart beating hard within my chest. "How about a donut?"

"Oh yeah, we've got those." The man says, nodding. "Apple fritter? Maple bar?"

I hesitate for a moment, not quite sure how to go about this. "Do you have anything a little… gayer?"

The man freezes for a moment, then glances around to make sure our small group of friends are the only people in the store. The coast is clear, but he still seem skeptical of me."

"Why would you think we had living gay donuts here?" The man asks.

HANDSOME SENTIENT FOOD POUNDS MY BUTT AND TURNS ME GAY

I'm not exactly sure how to play this, so I reluctantly decide to proceed with some honesty. "Well, there was that donut symbol on the window. Is that code?"

The guy shrugs. "Could be."

We stand here for a minute with the counter between use, neither one moving from our position.

"So... coffee then?" The man finally says.

I sigh, turning back around to face my friends but something stops me abruptly in my tracks. Adventure isn't about where you are, but who you are deep within. I could easily just call it a night right then and there, but at this moment I recognize that it's time to step up and make something happen. I turn back around.

"Listen." I say. "I know that there's a gay donut bar around here, and I may be a country boy but I'm not stupid. I might not have the password or whatever it is that you need me to say, but I recognize the symbol and I give you my word, I'm not a cop."

The guy behind the counter cracks a smile, amused by my sudden rush of confidence. "You're asking for someone else, right?" the guy ask with a slight twinkle in his eye.

"No." I respond, confused. Sam kicks me lightly in the shin.

"What was that? I couldn't hear you." The guy behind the counter continues. "Because most of the living donuts have moved back to Europe. The rest are in hiding, afraid of getting deported."

Sam seizes the moment and interjects. "We're wondering for some friends."

"Oh, well in that case I think I can do something for you!" The guy says, looking up with a wide smile and a wink. "I know some places. Actually, I might be about to help you out later tonight, have your friends call me."

"Really?" I blurt, unable to hide my excitement.

"I'm Parker." He says, handing me a card with his name, number, and that same mysterious round symbol.

"Mike." I tell him, "And this is Jordan and Sam."

"You know, the gay pastry scene isn't for everyone." Parker explains cryptically. "You gentlemen up for an adventure?"

"Of course," I smile. "It's exactly what we've been looking for."

After a few hours of getting ready I exchange some texts with Parker and we head out to meet him and some friends.

There is a thick excitement in the car as we cruise the city streets, looking for the mysterious address that I've been texted. Finally, something interesting is happening, a story in progress.

That tall-tale feeling is nothing but amplified when we arrive at the living donut bar, which Parker had insisted on calling a dessert speakeasy because there's a password at the door.

"Is this the place?" I ask an imposing man, bald and representing a similar love of tattoo's to Parker. It's hard to believe anything other than an industrial packing warehouse could be behind the door in question, but after double and triple checking the address, this is apparently the place.

"I don't know." The doorman says gruffly. "Is it?"

"The password." Sam reminds me.

"Oh yeah." I straighten myself out and stand up straight. "The password is 'Baker's dozen?'"

"Is that a question?" The doorman asks.

"Sorry." I try again. "Baker's dozen."

The imposing guy reaches over and twists the handle of the door, swinging it open to reveal a hustling, bustling donut shop within.

"Have fun boys." He says.

We step inside and make our way down the stairs. The place is hopping tonight, handsome men sipping on tall glasses of milk or coffee everywhere I look. Everyone here is much cooler than us Ohio.

"Mike!" A familiar voice shouts from somewhere near the bar. Out of the darkness comes Parker with a huge smile on his face, hugging all three of us in turn. "I'm so glad you guys could make it!"

"We're glad to be here!" I tell him. "This place is awesome."

Parker nods and then takes a long swing of his two percent milk.

Just then I notice a sign to the side of the band with glowing purple letters. It reads: The Big Glaze. Below it is a large doorway with two bouncers on either side, people are slowly filtering in.

"What's that?" I ask.

Parker laughs. "Order a milk first, then we'll talk."

After tossing back a few in a booth with Parker and his exceptionally cute friends I am practically boiling over with curiosity, but I hold my tongue. Everyone is having a great time, and the free drinks certainly don't make it easy to pace yourself. Finally, I just can't hold in my curiosity any longer.

"Alright dude." I brazenly interrupt the conversation that preceded me. "What's The Big Glaze?"

Parker takes a deep breath. "Okay, well." He starts. "This is a gay donut bar as you can see. Most of the gay donuts packed up and moved to Europe when they were outlawed, which is straight up unconstitutional if you ask me, but a few of them stayed behind. Now they live in hiding, but the donut community has found a way to let them work under the table, providing a particular service that is commonly referred to as glazing."

"What the fuck does that mean?" I finally ask. "I'm just a country boy from Ohio, you're gonna have to walk me through this."

Parker cracks a smile. "It means that one man is going to suck off a whole dozen gay donuts, and then they are going to glaze his face in hot, sugary cum."

Inside of me, a fire starts to burn, overtaking everything else with hot, unfiltered desire to be a part of this erotic celebration of living confectionery.

"A dozen?" I repeat back to Parker in astonishment. "That's a lot of glaze."

Parker nods. "Sometimes even more. The record right now is sixteen loads from sixteen different donuts. They've got chocolate, coconut, rainbow sprinkles, it's absolutely insane in there."

"That's..." I say, looking over at the door and reeling from all of the nasty thoughts that are suddenly filling my brain. "So hot." I finish.

My heart starts to race a mile a minute, almost pounding out of my chest with the realization that the adventure I'd been looking for has finally arrived. I don't think twice about what I say next, because I'm afraid that if I think too much I won't end up saying it. "Where do I sign up?"

Parker laughs. "Sign up to watch?"

I shake my head. "No. Sign up to perform."

When the lights go up on stage I find myself in a large, semi-circle theatre, with a wooden floor beneath me and a series of seats that tower upwards as they go. It's a steep incline and I'm at the bottom, looking up with my big green eyes as I rest on my knees. I've stripped down to nothing, my tan body and toned abs exposed to the audience. It's a full house tonight.

Thankfully, I'm too horny to be nervous, and my eyes dart about hungrily as I look for the sweet donut cocks that are apparently coming my way.

"Welcome to amateur night here at the downtown donut shop! Let's give it up for Mike!" A voice suddenly booms over the loudspeaker. "This is his first time here at The Big Glaze!"

The audience bursts into uproarious cheer and I can't help but smile, soaking it in.

"Remember," The voice continues. "The number of donut loads to beat without tapping out from exhaustion is fifteen. If Mike can take that, he'll receive The Big Glaze grand prize!"

More applause.

"Now let's get to it!" The voice finishes.

The next thing I know, a handsome, floating donut is approaching me from either side. The pastries are absolutely gorgeous, muscular and toned with massive dicks hanging down from their frosted, circular bodies.

I look up at them happily and take an engorged cock in each hand. They're well equipped, massively hung to the point that it's almost hard to wrap my fingers around their entire width. I try my best though, and soon I'm pumping up and down on each shaft expertly with my hands.

The audience seems to like what they see, and I notice a few of the watchers begin to stroke their own rods as the action unfolds before them.

Eventually, I start to use my tongue on each of the two sprinkled desserts, going from one to the other with quick licks from their balls to the tip. It's not long before I'm swallowing one of them entirely, pushing my head down onto his sweet, sugary cock and letting his length hit the threshold of my gag reflex. I choke and pull back, gasping for air as his member leaves my mouth in a trail of spit.

"One more time." I say, sheepishly.

"Yeah, suck that sprinkled cock." Says the donut in a sexy, authoritative tone. "You like that sweetness don't you?"

I devour his giant cock once more, but this time I relax as it hits the back of my throat and end up taking him entirely to the base. My face is pressed up against his pink frosting as his dick hits its limit, then he starts fucking my face hard.

The donut plows into me, pumping up and down and using me like a gay human sex toy, which actually starts to make me hard down below. While he enjoys my mouth, I make sure to continue stroking the other dessert on stage and he seems to appreciate it, finding a rhythm with his movement against my steady strokes.

With my free hand I reach down and start to play with my cock, massaging myself as I'm violated by the living junk food.

The stage lights feel bright on my skin, completely exposed to the crowd before me. My friends are out there watching, Parker too, and exposing myself to them like this is potently arousing. I have never been so horny in my entire life, consumed by the taboo nature of this human on pastry encounter.

Eventually, the floating donuts on either side of me start to tremble with pleasure, edging closer and closer to orgasm. I pick up the pace, using the spit from my mouth to frantically beat them off until finally they explode across my face in tandem. Two hot white loads fly through the air in milky ropes, splattering across my cheeks from ear to ear. I open my mouth to catch some of the liquid, and then swallow hungrily as the desserts disappear back into the darkness with drained balls.

Immediately, two freshly baked maple bars approach me, taking their friend's place. These pastries are equally hung, and with a newfound ferocity and a face full of cum I start to expertly suck them off. The desserts are clearly enjoying themselves, roughly passing me back and forth between them.

I swallow deep. The maple bar to my left takes me all the way down and gags me, brutally pushing me to the point that I'm unable to breathe around the girth of his enormous dick. My tongue pushes out from the bottom of his shaft and laps against his syrupy balls as I choke.

"Of fuck." The living confectionery starts to moan from his single, circular opening. "Are you ready for one more?"

I pull back to answer, but before I can form the words a warm blast of jizz hits me in the face. I laugh a little as it somehow manages to get up my nose, and I smile when the strings of semen dangle off of me. He pumps a few more shots and then turns me to face the other sweet treat, who's balls I massage in my hand.

"Cover my fucking face with your sugary frosting." I beg, starting to get into it now. "Use me as your gay donut cum dumpster."

He begins to moan and shake, bucking foreword and releasing his tension in the form of hot splatters across my face.

Now that I've got four loads to contend with, I'm finally starting to feel the jizz blend together and form a thin sheen of glazed icing across my face. It's like wearing a mask at the spa, only warmer and many times more explicit. A little bit of it has managed to end up near my eyes and I wipe it away with my fingers, blinking rapidly and looking up at the group of hard cocked donuts that now float around me. Seeing that I can hold my own out here, the group has given up on approaching two by two and instead have formed a tight circle with me as the centerpiece.

I look up at them with pleading eyes, making my way around the circle with both hands while I ache to be touched myself.

Soon this new group of desserts begins to pop, a spray here and a splatter there. They fling ropes of semen at me from every direction, landing them expertly across my face. From chin to forehead I'm covered in pearly white milk, which runs down my neck and across my chest in long drips. Dots of white speckle my eyelashes, which I fight desperately to see through as the donuts come and go above me.

I have no idea how many loads I've taken until finally the announcer booms over the loudspeaker once again.

"Nice work!" The voice bellows. "Mike has reached ten loads of hot, steamy frosting! That's nearly a dozen!"

The audience bursts into uproarious applause and I smile wide as the strands that dangle from my chin dance in the air. I continue to stroke my dick and as I do my body tenses up with aching warmth, overwhelmed by the depraved situation that I have somehow gotten myself into.

"He's only got six more to go before winning tonight's grand prize! Where are those loads going to be?"

Suddenly, on stage right, a huge wheel lights up and starts to spin. I can barely make out the words that are printed on it, but it appears to be a list of different body parts; mouth, abs, chest. Someone hands me a small buzzer with a single red button on top and I hold it for a moment, not entirely sure what to do next, until finally I decide that my only option is to push it. The wheel begins to slow to a crawl and as it does our audience cheers, clearly thrilled about the impending result. When the wheel comes to a complete stop, the whole place erupts.

"Alright!" The announcer calls in a long drawl. "The final six frosting loads will be blasted onto Mike's tight gay asshole!"

Two stagehands approach and help lean me back onto the ground, then position some sort of ramp under me so that my legs are lifted and slowly placed behind my head. My upper back still on the wooden stage floor, I find myself with my ass in the air and my butthole completely exposed to the world.

Two floating donuts approach me with their cocks in their tiny baked hands, beating off and looking down at my fit body as it lies contorted below them. One of them is covered in dark brown chocolate sprinkles while the other sports an incredibly arousing coat of coconut shavings.

The first treat starts to moan almost immediately and shoots a string of semen directly into my asshole, where it lands and pools for a moment before sliding back down the crack of my ass. The next follows closely behind, but his aim is a little off so his jizz flies onto my butt, but also somehow manages to add a few splatters to the mess on my face.

"Eleven!" The announcer calls out. "Twelve!"

Two more frozed treats approach and position themselves accordingly. As they pleasure themselves I do the same, spastically rubbing my cock while I tiptoe on the edge of pure, blissful orgasm.

As the donuts blow their loads I finally cum myself, the muscles in my stomach contracting wildly as wave after wave of pleasure shoots through me. I scream a wild, animalistic yelp and let go of everything, my eyes rolling back into my head like a man possessed. I can feel the cum frosting raining down onto me as I tremble and quake, my body disappearing somehow and leaving me as an object of pure blinding pleasure. The sensation envelopes me as jizz continues to fall and the announcer calls out my benchmarks. My own load spurts back across the stage is a forceful blast.

"Thriteen!" He says. "Fourteen! Fifteen!"

I'm not even aware that the desserts have been replaced by others because my eyes are now completely caked shut with sugary semen.

"Sixteen!" The announcer crows and the audience loses their minds.

I collapse back only the stage floor and the ramp is pulled out from under me so that I can lay flat. I'm utterly glazed with donut semen.

"We have a winner!" The voice says. "Tell him what he's won!"

Another voice suddenly comes over the loudspeaker, higher pitched and speaking rapidly like I'm trapped in some sort of bizarre sexual infomercial.

"Well Mike, you've had a great night here on The Big Glaze, starring in your very own donut show and taking sixteen loads! You're going to love taking sixteen more during your all expenses paid trip to Holland, home of the Dutch who came to America and invented the donut many, many years ago! You'll stay at the finest luxury hotel that Holland has to offer before being whisked away to our sister donut shop for your very own headline show!"

The crowd cheers again and I smile, sensing through the layers of cum on my closed eyelids that the stage curtain is now closing. I lay alone in the darkness, slowly trying to recover from the best night of my life.

SLAMMED UP THE BUTT BY MY HOT COFFEE BOSS

From the very second I step foot into the office, I know that something here is different. It's not any specific detail that gives it away, no single glaring sign that blinks above the doorway screaming for my attention. Instead, I recognize it in the weight of the air, the way that it feels against my skin when I walk through the lobby of our modest commercial building on the north side of town.

I stop, and suddenly it hits me, the strong scent of coffee.

I hear footsteps approaching down the hallway and moments later my coworker, Janet, rounds the corner. She smiles and waves as she sees me, but I can tell there is something slightly off about her.

"Did you hear?" Janet asks, halting in front of me.

I shake my head. "Hear what?"

"Brickle got fired over the weekend." Janet replies.

Darpo Brickle was my boss, and despite his tendency to be a bit of a hard ass, the guy was a great leader and pretty fun to be around. I had no idea about his termination, but I also can't say that the news comes as that much of a surprise. Sales had been lagging a lot lately, and despite Darpo's efforts to get the team back on track, things haven't exactly been looking up around the office lately.

"What happened?" I ask.

"The higher ups wanted him gone." Janet tells me. "Apparently, his performance ratings we're through the floor, just terrible numbers this quarter."

I shake my head. "That's too bad, I actually liked the guy."

"Well, you're really gonna miss him once you meet the replacement." Janet says, and then suddenly straightens up. "That reminds me, I was just grabbing something out of my car but there's a meeting in the conference room in five minutes. Don't be late."

I glance at my watch. "Already? It's so early."

"He's already kicking things into high gear." Janet tells me as she walks past and heads out into the parking lot.

I watch my coworker go for a moment and then heed her warning, kicking my pace into double time as I continue down the hallway and then up the stairs towards our large corner office.

When I push open the door I find the usual hustling and bustling rows of cubicles completely empty, instead noticing that the conference room is in full swing. I immediately head over and push my way inside, finding my way through the usual suit and tie crowd until I arrive at an empty folding chair and sit.

"He's coming!" Someone suddenly says, causing the entire room of people to quiet down and find their seats.

Moments later, the door to the conference room opens and a massive, piping-hot cup of coffee comes sliding in across the carpet. He's tall, around six-and-a-half feet, and quite handsome for a beverage, wearing a tie around his ceramic body and sporting a large, muscular handle. I can't help letting my breath catch in my throat, not expecting to be so enchanted by this man, not only because he is a cup of coffee, but because I consider myself to be totally straight.

Still, my attraction to this powerful java cannot be denied.

"Some of you have already met me, and some of you have not, so let's get this out of the way right now." Says the coffee. "My name is Morcho Kibclaw, and I'm your new boss."

The coffee scans the room after he says this, as if trying to pick up on any subtle reactions to this statement of introduction. He's like a shark in the deep black ocean, sniffing around for the scent of blood in the water.

"Your old boss, Mr. Brickle, wasn't cutting it around here." Morcho continues. "Can anyone tell me how Brickle wasn't cutting it?"

There is silence for a moment and then a single hand goes up. It's my co-worker, Danny.

"Yes?" The coffee says, nodding in his direction.

HANDSOME SENTIENT FOOD POUNDS MY BUTT AND TURNS ME GAY

"He wasn't hitting his numbers." Says Danny. "Sales were down."

The coffee cup seems impressed with this answer. "That's correct. We are business of numbers, all right? And Brickle must have forgotten that along the way because, despite the bad numbers, he was still granting time off and allowing people to leave early. That's not the kind of company we are going to run anymore here at Parkoon Lances. Would you like to know what kind of lance company we are going to be?"

Another hand slowly goes up.

"Yes?" Morcho asks.

"The one with the best customer care in the tri-cities area?" Answers my co-worker, Bill, with a lack of confidence that makes me cringe.

The imposing coffee cup sits in absolute silence for a moment, his expression utterly void of any warning at what's to come.

Suddenly, Morcho speaks. "Get the fuck out."

Bill looks utterly stunned and somewhat confused. "What?"

"I said get the fuck out." Repeats the coffee cup.

"Are you serious?" Laughs my co-worker, clearly not wanting to accept his rather brutal fate.

Suddenly, the coffee cup slides forward through the rows of folding chairs, knocking them this way and that and causing people to jump out of the way before getting roughly bowled over by the ceramic mug. A few people cower in terror while others scream, but Morcho ignores them and, the next thing I know, the massive coffee cup is towering over Bill, looking down at him with a searing vengeance unlike anything that I have ever seen.

"You're fucking fired." The coffee cup yells. "Now get the fuck out of my sight before I pour myself all over you."

Bill stands up and grabs his coat, crying, then stumbles over to the door, pushing out into the main office as tears stream down his face.

"The answer is simple." Announces Morcho to the room. "What kind of lance company are we going to be? The best fucking lance company on the planet. The next person who talks to me about customer service like I give a damn is going to get hot coffee all over their lap, is that understood?"

Morcho slides back across the room and positions himself in front of the crowd once again, while my coworkers struggle to turn their folding chairs upright and reorganize.

"As you can see." Morcho says. "I don't have time for any of your bullshit. Today, I want you all working twice as hard as you normally would. Birthday coming up? Why not get your kid a lance? Horse show? How about some jousting? We've got lances for that. If I come around and you're not on the phone selling somebody a brand new pointy lance then your ass is grass, understood?"

"Yes." The entire conference room repeats back to Morcho in unison.

Suddenly, the door opens and Janet strolls in, stopping suddenly when she sees the chaos that has occurred. She looks to Morcho, "Sorry I'm late, I was just getting some papers out of my car."

There is an audible gasp as the entire room holds their breath, waiting on the edge of our seats in preparation for Morcho's reaction to Janet's tardiness.

The coffee cup hesitates for a moment and then slides over to Janet, ever so slowly. I can hardly watch, struggling not to literally avert my eyes as the mug drifts closer and closer to my unfortunate friend.

"You're not late." Says Morcho, sitting just inches away from Janet's face now. "How can you be late if you don't work here anymore."

Janet looks confused. "What?"

Morcho hesitates and then suddenly he's flipping himself upside down in one swift motion. It entire room jumps in surprise as Morcho goes spilling everywhere, the hot coffee cascading down and covering Janet from head to toe as she screams. The liquid pools out across the floor and Janet begins belligerently crying, lucky that Morcho is cooler than the steam rising off of his top would have you believe.

"Get out!" The coffee bellows, oozing into the carpet with every passing second. "Get the fuck out and never come back!"

Janet turns and rushes out of the room, her entire body stained brown from the hot liquid.

"Meeting's over!" Screams Morcho. "Now get back to work! I'll be pulling you in one by one for individual meetings over the next hour, and if I don't like what I hear from you then you can expect to end up just like her!"

Nobody moves a muscle, unsure of whether or not this terrifying beverage has actually excused us.

"Go!" Yells Morcho. "Get out!"

Everyone bursts up from their chair and hurries out of the room, careful not to step on the new boss as be begins to collect himself back

HANDSOME SENTIENT FOOD POUNDS MY BUTT AND TURNS ME GAY

within the massive cup.

The rest of the day I am on pins and needles, working harder than I ever have since first starting this job a year ago. Every single call that I make feels like it's life or death which, I suppose, means that the coffee cup's aggressive style of management is actually working. In the cubicles around me, I can hear my coworkers typing and talking with equal fervor, trying every tactic in the book to get out there and sell more lances.

One by one, people start getting called into Morcho's office, where the blinds have been menacingly drawn. The meetings seem relatively short, and consistently result in one of two endings.

Half of the group comes out and walks back to their desk, clearly shaken up but otherwise happy to remain employed. The other half, however, aren't so lucky.

There is a loud crash as the door to Morcho's office opens up and Danny comes stumbling out, tears streaming down his face as the coffee shouts angrily at him in the background. A chair suddenly comes flying out of the office door after him, narrowly missing the man as it clatters along the hallway with a second, even louder crash.

"And don't come back!" Morcho screams. There is a moment of silence, and then suddenly the moment I had been dreading all morning finally arrives. "Yonce Peppers!" Screams Morcho.

I stand. "Coming!"

The entire office stares as I make my way through the rows towards the gaping office door, a collective tension surging through the air like an electrical current.

I arrive at Morcho's office and step inside.

"Close the door behind you." Says the cup from behind his desk. Darpo's computer has already been removed, replaced by a station for sugar, cream and artificial sweetener.

I close the door.

"Have a seat." Morcho offers, motioning to the empty chair that sits across from him. I feel as though I'm being directed to the gallows, but I have no other option than to obey the commands of my ruthless liquid boss. I sit carefully, trying not to show my nervousness but unable to keep my body from trembling ever so slightly.

I can tell by the way this muscular coffee cup eyes me up that he notices, but he says nothing.

"Tell me, Yonce. Why did you get into the lance business?" Questions the new boss.

Immediately, my head is swimming with any number of possible answers. The obvious way to play it is to make up some kind of story in which lances mean the world to me, maybe my father was a huge lance enthusiast and raised me on our farm tossing them around in the Midwest. But, of course, that would be a lie.

The real answer is that I took the job because I need the money, as blunt as that may be, and I just so happen to be really good at it.

I swallow hard, and make my choice.

"I'm not going to lie." I tell the beautiful, yet utterly terrifying, coffee. "I started working here out of necessity, I needed the job and I really don't care about lances."

"I find that hard to believe." Scoffs Morcho, glancing down at a piece of paper on his desk. "It says here that you're from Florida, lance capital of the world."

I shrug. "I know. It's hard to believe, but I've just never understood the appeal. I'm more of a pitchfork or trident man myself, but I think that's what makes me so good at this job. I truly understand the competition."

The second that these words leave my mouth I can see something in the coffee cups demeanor change. He instantly relaxes, softens even, and I feel ever so slightly more at ease. Now that I'm no longer completely terrified of the beverage, I can definitely feel that same aching attraction begin to seep into my thoughts.

"I like that answer." Says Morcho. "It's honest, and that's something we need around here. Too many people are here because they said the right thing at the right time, not because they actually bring anything real to the table."

The massive coffee cup reaches down and takes a sugar packet off of the desk in front of him, tearing open the edge and pouring it over the top of his head.

"So tell me." The beverage begins. "What do you bring to the table?"

I immediately notice something strange about the way my boss says this, a slight inflection that, if I didn't know any better, might have come off as flirtatious. Of course, that can't possibly be the case so I answer him straightly.

"I'm the best that there is as far as developing repeat business from our clients." I explain. "I know exactly how to keep them involved with us, whether it's setting up lance parties or just getting out there and making house calls to our biggest lance buyers."

The coffee eyes me up and down. "Another good answer." He observes. "You really know your stuff."

"Thank you, sir." I say with a nod.

"What do you know about living coffee?" Asks Morcho.

This feels like a loaded question, so I tread carefully. "Well, I know that you're brewed locally most of the time."

Morcho nods.

"House blend?" I ask.

"Kona." Morcho tells me. "But that's very flattering."

Once more I can feel the surge of erotic tension between us, and once more I try my best to ignore it.

Morcho clears his throat. "Something you might not know about living coffee is that it is very important for us to regulate our heat. As you can see, I'm very, very large. I can't fit in a microwave to be reheated over and over again."

"What kind of heat do you need?" I ask.

Morcho lets a smug grin cross his ceramic face. "Erotic heat."

My heart almost stops as he says this, not sure whether this explanation is a joke or a deadly serious fact of the living coffee lifestyle. Thinking quickly, I decide that it's safest to go with the serious approach.

"And that works?" I ask with as much genuine curiosity as I can muster.

Morcho nods. "Not only does it work, but it's very, very important. Without erotic heat I could eventually turn lukewarm and die."

In this moment I am actually struck with a touch of sympathy for my ruthless leader. If *I* was constantly hovering so close to deaths door, I would probably be a little upset, too, and I certainly wouldn't have any time to deal with people who didn't take their job seriously. With every second my heart is growing larger and larger for Morcho, and I'm both scared and excited by the prospect. I realize suddenly that my cock has grown hard within my slacks, a physical representation of my swelling admiration for this handsome cup of coffee.

"Corporate has given me permission to hire on an employee to keep me warm." Morcho explains. "They will be given a raise, of course. I'd like to hire you on for this position."

"Me?" I ask, stunned. "Why me?"

"I'd like to say it's because you have all the right answers." Replies Morcho. "But in reality, it's because you're just so fucking sexy."

I blush, trying to hide the fact that his blunt admission turns me on even more.

"I've never been with a living coffee." I admit.

"Any other living beverage?" Morcho asks, curiously.

I think for a moment. "A gang of chocolate milk cowboys once." I tell him. "But that was in another life, I must have pressed the button nearly forty times since then."

Morcho nods in understanding. "Well I can promise you this, I've got much more to offer than just a boring old chocolate milk."

The large mug of coffee seductively begins to slide around the desk towards me, moving quietly across the carpet until he is right up next to my chair where I can now feel the pleasant heat radiating off of him. The beverage smells incredible, perfectly brewed.

"There's one more thing." I say, stopping my boss in his tracks. "I'm not gay."

"Everyone's gay for coffee." Morcho says, pulling me close to him and kissing me deeply.

My first instinct is to pull away, but I immediately recognize this response for what it is, the irrational fear of a truth that I know at the bottom of my heart is real. I want this cup of coffee and I want him badly.

"I accept." I tell the cup in between wild kisses of passion. "I accept the job as your erotic heater."

"Good." Morcho says. "Now get to work."

Seized with an incredible gay lust, I immediately drop to my knees before this giant cup, happy to discover that a massive erect cock has risen out of his body and now stands at full attention before me.

I look up at Morcho, impressed. "This is going to be fun." I say.

I open wide and take the coffee's dick deep into my throat, pumping my head across the length of his shaft in a series of slow, deliberate movements. My boss moans with pleasure, tilting his head back and bubbling a little at the top.

I reach up with one hand and being to play with his hanging coffee balls then, moments later, push down as far as I can, taking his entire length within me. Somehow I manage to relax enough to allow the beverage well past my gag reflex, my face pressed hard against the cup's ceramic abs.

Morcho reaches down and holds me here for a moment, enjoying the sensation of having me consume his shaft fully, the entirely of his rod lodged deep within my neck. I force my tongue out as far as I can and tickle the edge of his balls playfully until finally there's just not enough air left in my lungs and I pull back in a massive gasp.

Spit hangs between my lips and the head of his shaft in a single, thick rope, which I immediately use as lube while I beat the coffee boss off furiously. Faster and faster I go, pleasuring him with everything I've got until finally I just can't take it any longer, standing abruptly.

"I need you inside of me." I admit to the handsome beverage. "I need to deep inside this gay ass and I need it now. Punish me like I just came in late for work."

"You want me to spill on you?" Morcho asks. "Like Janet?"

I shake my head. "No, punish me with your fat beverage dick."

My boss smiles and nods. "With pleasure."

I immediately step past him and unbutton my pants, pulling them down along with my underwear and then leaning over his large wooden desk. I reach back with one hand and spread myself open for him, then wink coyly. "Pound me."

The massive coffee cup gladly slides into position and begins to align the head of his swollen dick with my puckered tightness, teasing the rim of my ass with his massive length.

"Do it!" I demand. "Shove it in there and fuck the hell out of me like the bad little twink that I am."

Morcho slams forward, stuffing me completely with his utterly enormous rod and causing me to yelp out loudly in a mixture of both pain and pleasure. I grip onto the desk tightly as my boss begins to thrust within me, moving slowly at first and then building speed. It feels utterly incredible, a sensation unlike anything I have ever felt, complete with a slight buzz from the rectally consumed caffeine high.

"Fuck!" I moan, biting my lip as Morcho's cock brutally impales me. "It feels so fucking good getting slammed up the ass by my coffee in the morning."

The coffee continues to pound me like this for quite a while, hammering away at my asshole with powerful, rhythmic force. I reach down between my legs and grab ahold of my hanging cock beneath, stroking pleasantly in time with every thrust up my rear.

It's not long before the pleasant sensations of prostate orgasm begins to build within me, a strange and unfamiliar warmth that slowly but surely starts to creep through my body, beginning deep within my abdomen and then sweeping down across my arms and legs. I am trembling, quaking with pleasure, unable to entirely process the feelings that course through me and letting the excess come out in an expression of uncontrollable shaking.

"I'm gonna blow my load so fucking hard!" I cry out.

My huge coffee boss immediately stops, pulling out of me and slapping my rear. "No, you're not." The beverage says. "I'm not warm enough."

"I'm sorry, sir." I tell him. "I'll cum when you tell me to."

"Good." Replies the liquid. "That's what I like to hear."

Morcho grabs me around the waist and then flips me over on the desk so that I'm laying on my back. He grabs my pants and underwear, tearing them down and then ripping them off completely so that my asshole and hard cock are exposed to him. My muscular legs splayed wide, the giant coffee cup aligns his cock with my now reamed backdoor and pushes forward, stretching out my tightness with his incredible girth.

I can now feel the heat within my boss radiating against me much stronger than before, the cup of coffee clearly getting the change in temperature that he so desperately craved.

As Morcho slams into me once again, I start to beg for what I crave, sweet release.

"Please let me cum!" I beg. "Please let me blow this fucking load."

Morcho pounds me up the ass like a java jackhammer, ignoring my words.

"I need to cum! I'm begging you!" I moan, the caffeine surging through me.

"We'll cum together." Morcho suddenly announces.

I reach down and begin beating myself of frantically, finally allowing the sensation of orgasm to completely consume my body. I close my eyes tight as it hits me in a sensual wave that pulses through my body over and over again, each one more powerful than the next until finally I throw my head back and scream, a fountain of white hot jizz ejecting from the head of my cock.

"Oh fuck!" Morcho cries out, clearly finding himself in the midst of a similar experience. The muscular beverage slams into me deep and holds, his arms trembling as he braces against the tidal wave of pleasure and then finally releasing as his cum spills out into my rectum. I can feel him filling me with load after aching load, the spunk pouring out from my boss until finally there's just no more room in my asshole to hold him. The jizz comes spilling down my legs and crack in pearly white streaks.

When Morcho finally pulls out of me completely, the rest of his load goes with him, splattering onto the desk below.

"That was perfect." Says Morcho, reaching out a hand and helping me up as his cum continues to drip from my reamed ass. "Looks like you're just the man I was looking for."

"I won't let you down." I tell my boss confidently, then hesitate. "But there's something else."

"What is it?" Morcho asks, his harsh exterior completely melted away now to reveal a strong, sensitive man underneath.

I'm struggling to find my words, overwhelmed with emotion as I process the events of the last forty-five minutes. "I... I..."

Morcho slides up against me and lets me feel his pleasant heat across my skin.

"I think I love you." I finally say. "I don't want this meeting to end, I don't want to ever be without you by my side."

"I love you, too." Says Morcho.

We hold each other for quite a while, standing naked in the middle of Morcho's office until eventually he speaks again. "You know, you don't have to leave if you don't want to."

I look up at my boss, confused. "What do you mean?"

"I mean we can be together forever, if that's truly what you want." The coffee explains. "All you have to do is climb inside of me."

"Climb inside of you?" I repeat back in utter shock. "But it's hot! What will happen to me?"

"Well, it's going to feel very, very strange, but eventually you'll turn into coffee, too." Morcho says. "We'll be together forever."

"But who will keep you warm?" I ask.

"We'll find someone." Morcho assures me.

Overwhelmed by my love for this incredible beverage, I climb up onto his desk, standing so that I can look down into the massive brown pool that waits between the cup's ceramic edges. The prospect of climbing in is terrifying, but the prospect of spending a single second of my life without Morcho is even worse.

"Okay." I say. "Let's do it."

I take a deep breath and then throw one leg over the edge, wincing from the heat. It's very warm, but not painful; actually quite pleasant in a way. I throw my other leg over the edge and now, sitting on the side, I close my eyes, enjoying the powerful java scent that permeates everything around us.

I slip off of the edge and disappear into the swirling pool of delicious coffee.

OPPRESSED IN THE BUTT BY MY INCLUSIVE HOLIDAY COFFEE CUPS

If there is one thing that I love about the Christmas season, it's buying things. Not necessarily giving them away, either, because even though gifts are wonderful, they can't compare to the sensual pulse of a credit card swipe through a virgin machine. It's truly beautiful and, besides Santa Clause, the tree, and my boy J.C., it's what the season is all about.

Sometimes during Christmastime (which officially starts on the first of October as far as I'm concerned), I'll cruise out to the mall and just sit there in the food court, taking it all in. At first, there's not much to see, the usual comings and goings of a typical American town, but as the days drift further and further into November and then finally December, everything changes.

December, or as I like to call it, The Big Show, is when the string lighting starts making its first appearance, the trees start lifting high into the sky and the carolers begin to shout out from high on the rooftops, harkening down as I spend and spend and spend.

Last year, I spent so much time out there at the mall that my wife Susan had to take me in to the local hospital for severe dehydration and malnourishment. I swore that, from that day onward, I would make sure to break sometimes for eggnog and ginger bread houses, and my wife was satisfied with that.

This year, I've been good about taking care of myself, pounding eggnog until the cows come home.

To be honest, however, I'm about ready to switch over to my favorite treat, Christmas blend coffee from Starbutts.

I have a rule when it comes to holiday coffee; I refuse to buy it until they bring out the bright red cups.

You know the ones that I'm talking about, right? Those wonderfully festive little gems that depict the Christmas season in all of its glory, complete with decorative pines, mistletoe, reindeers and even St. Nick himself.

It gives me a rock hard erection just thinking about it.

The thing is, I just can't tolerate having my Christmas blend coffee in a plain cup, so I refuse to drink it until Starbutts, my favorite coffee shop, marches out the red cups on November first.

Now here I am on the eve of the big red reveal, camped outside of my local Starbutts. While other's like to celebrate this evening by dressing up in costumes, stealing candy and hailing the dark lord Satan with his heathen tradition known as Halloween, I have dedicated my time to making darn sure that I'm the first in line when that cup of hot Christmas blend comes out.

My name is gonna be on that cup.

One of the Starbutts employees spots me sitting outside and opens the front door, sticking her head out into the chilly evening air. "Oh, I'm sorry, sir," she says, "we're already closed tonight."

"Oh, I know," I inform her, "I'm just here for the cups."

The woman looks confused. "Excuse me?"

"The cups," I repeat, "I'm just here for the holiday cups tomorrow, I wanted to be the first in line."

Her look of confusion slowly turns to one of amusement.

"You know, I don't think we're going to run out of cups," the woman informs me, "there's plenty to go around."

I nod. "But I need to get there first, you know? Get into the Christmas spirit?"

"Sure," the woman says. She turns to head back inside and then stops herself, turning around and poking her head out into the night air once again. "Are you sure you're going to be okay out here? It's supposed to drop below zero tonight, might even get some snow."

"Even better," I say, nodding to her as I wrap my blanket even tighter around myself, "even better."

The young woman shrugs and then heads back inside, locking the door behind her as she finishes closing down shop for the evening.

I shut my eyes tight and settle in, ready to prove to the world that I am one with the Christmas spirit, a perfect solider of holiday glee who is ready to do battle in the name of Yuletide cheer.

Visions of sugarplums dance in my head as I try my best to snooze, the frosty air nipping at my nose until, finally, all of my senses seem to fade away into a big black nothingness.

The next thing I know, I'm floating through a vivid dream world, high above the city as I gaze down upon the houses below. I'm looking out over the edge of a sleigh several that is miles up in the sky, and sitting next to me are both Jesus and Santa Clause, each of them incredibly ripped and shirtless.

Nice.

"Where are we going?" I ask.

"To the place where all men reverse themselves," the two of them tell me in unison.

I have no idea what this means, but I suddenly feel slightly unsettled. There is something about this that doesn't seem quite right, the edges of my dream beginning to peel back and reveal a haunting nightmare underneath the polished exterior.

Suddenly, the sleigh dips sharply and we are plummeting down towards the earth below, the icy air whipping up across my face with a wild fury.

"Oh my god!" I cry out, gripping tightly onto the wood in front of me as I try my best not to fly out.

At this point I am certain that these are my final breaths, screaming at the top of my lungs until suddenly, at the very last minute, the sleigh pulls back and we land ever so softly outside of the very same Starbutts that I fell asleep at. Now, however, the business is absolutely packed with people, overflowing with customers as they scramble to claim decorative red cups of their own.

Jesus and Santa Clause climb out of the sleigh and then turn back to face me. "Follow us," they command in unison.

I do as I'm told, climbing up off of my wooden bench and stepping out into the sprawling mass of frantic customers.

Jesus and Santa lead the way, parting the crowd as they hold up official Christmas lanyards, which are clearly labeled 'all access.'

"I'm with them," I offer the disappointed patrons who shoot me fierce glares of anger while I slink past the pack, pushing forward until finally the three of us find ourselves pressed up against the Starbutts counter.

"What can I get started for you?" a handsome, bearded employee asks me.

Before I have a chance to respond, Jesus and Santa Clause interject on my behalf. "Reindeer milk," the two of them announce.

"Very good," the man behind the counter says, turning away to begin my beverage.

"I was just hoping to get a cup of the Christmas blend," I stammer, but Jesus and Santa Clause ignore me completely.

Moments later, the bearded man turns around and hands me a bright red Starbutts cup. I stare down at it, my brain struggling to grapple with the absolutely horrific image that fills my field of vision. From afar this would appear to be your typical Starbutts Christmas goblet, but in some disgusting, nightmarish trick, all of the jolly, holiday imagery has been wiped away and removed completely.

"What is this?" I stammer, my heartbeat kicking into double time as cold sweat forms across my brow.

"Reindeer blood," the bearded barista replies, his eyes now completely black.

The next thing I know, the entire building is melting around me in a mixture of hellish red, the nightmare finally revealing itself in all of its terrifying glory. Flames erupt from every side, and when I spin around I see that Santa Clause is now a giant, generic holiday snowflake while Jesus has transformed into an enormous Star of David.

"Noooooo!" I scream out, tilting my head back and erupting with a howl of pure anguish.

Suddenly, I bolt upright, the surreal dream disappearing as reality returns and hits me hard in the chest. I take a deep breath, overwhelmed with gratitude that this horrible experience had been nothing more than a holiday dream.

I find myself sitting in exactly the same spot on the sidewalk, right outside of Starbutts, only now the first cracks of sunlight are creeping their way across the horizon of the distant, snow covered mountains.

There is a loud click as the door next to me unlocks, and I glance over to see the same young woman who spoke to me last night opening up for the early shift.

Immediately, I turn to look behind me, expecting to find the same massive swarms lining up behind me in a sea of chaos, just like in the dream. This prediction couldn't be farther from the truth, however, as the only thing that has appeared behind me over night is a light layer of frost across the sidewalk.

I stand up, slightly confused but still grateful to call myself the first in line for this season's incredibly important red Starbutts cups.

"Come on in," says the young woman, "we're open."

I excitedly push past her, making my way through the door and then rushing up to the front of the counter so fast my backwards baseball cap nearly flies off of my head.

"Christmas blend!" I shout.

Moments later, the barista appears at the register, somewhat taken aback by my excitement and enthusiasm.

"That will be two dollars," she tells me.

I pull out the crumbled bills and place them on the counter, my entire body trembling as I attempt to contain my excitement for this thrilling tradition to unfold.

My mind races with what kind of beautiful Christmas imagery could be depicted across the seasonal red cups, what kind of gorgeous Christian iconography is in store for my unprepared, moral mind to experience?

Personally, I have my fingers crossed for eleven lords a' leaping, but only time will tell.

Soon enough, the young woman returns with my coffee, piping hot in its beautiful red cup. I take the beverage from her and look down, ready for anything but never expecting what lies before me.

My breath immediately catches in my throat as a cold jolt of panic surges through me. Am I still dreaming? Is this my nightmare?

The cup that I hold in my hands is certainly the traditional Starbutts red, but that is precisely where the Christmas spirit ends.

The cup is a blank, matte crimson from top to bottom.

Without even thinking I drop the cup, which explodes in a flurry of hot black coffee across the floor. My heart is slamming hard in my chest, thundering through me with a rapid pound as I struggle to collect my senses. Everything is spinning, the entire room shifting as my knees buckle and give out below me.

Suddenly, I open my eyes to find that I'm strapped to a table with a bright light shining above me.

"Oh, thank god," I blurt, "it was just another dream."

"Afraid not," comes a voice from somewhere off to the side.

I try to glance over but immediately realize I am securely fastened to the table below.

"Where am I?" I question.

The next thing I know, a nurse is leaning over me, looking down with an expression of grave concern on her face. "You had a nasty fall in Starbutts," the woman explains. "You passed out and hit your head on the counter."

"I did?" I ask her, completely shocked by this revelation.

"You did," the nurse assures me with a nod. "I'm Nurse Keenankel, do you remember what your name is?"

I suddenly realize that I have no idea.

"Well, we called your wife because you had an ID in your pocket," the nurse informs me, "so you'll be happy to know that your name is Jabua Fogstein and you're a former preacher, does that ring any bells?"

"If I'm a former preacher what do I do now?" I ask.

"Your wife tells us that you spend most of the year making videos for the Internet and preparing for Starbutts Christmas cups," the nurse reveals.

Suddenly, I'm reminded of exactly how I ended up here, my entire body seizing as my heart kicks into double time at the thought of Starbutts cups turning plain matte red this season.

A loud beeping staccato erupts from the room around me, which I now realize is the inside of an ambulance. My entire body is shaking and convulsing wildly, threatening to break loose from the tight leather straps that wrap across me.

"He's going into cardiac arrest!" the nurse screams, prompting another one of the medical technicians to appear above me. "We're losing him!"

Keenankel grabs a set of paddles from the wall and rubs them together as a high pitched whine fills my ears, then she slams them down against my chest as a blinding jolt of electricity surges through me.

I shake in one powerful convulsion, then suddenly I find myself breathing normally once more, calm and collected as I settle back against my gurney.

"Mr. Fogstein," the nurse says, "you can't keep reacting like this every time you think about these Starbucks cups, it's not healthy."

She's right, and I know it, but I just can't help the way that I feel. I try my best to fight it, but soon a cascade of tears is welling up within my eyes and then spilling down over the edge of them, streaking my cheeks with their salty wetness.

"I know," I tell her, blubbering like a child. "I know, but I can't help it, these cups mean so much to me."

"But why?" the nurse begs to know, trying to understand the utter horror that I am going through.

"Because they're trying to boycott Christmas!" I tell her. "Starbutts is trying to make this season for everyone instead of just for Christians. They're oppressing me!"

"Well, I mean, does it really matter what the cup looks like?" Keenankel asks. "It's just a cup."

"Yes, it matters," I retort, "I didn't expect you to understand. These are my Christmas cups! Don't you understand that? Christmas is the only time that us Christians are not an oppressed minority and now they're trying to take that away from us, too!"

"I don't know about that," the nurse says skeptically.

"It's true!" I tell her. "You'll never understand until you've lived it, but it's absolutely true and it's not fair!"

"Well alright, sir," Keenankel offers, "let's just try not to get so worked up about the cups, though, okay? We don't want you to hurt yourself."

After my episode, I spend the next two days in the hospital under heavy observation. Everyone is gravely concerned, family, friends and fans, especially when I make a viral video to express my displeasure with the new Starbutts changes.

Suddenly, supporters are coming out of the woodwork, telling me that they to are disappointed with the Starbutts decided to make their business a place of inclusion and harmony.

I feels great to have this much of a passionate team behind me, but as I lay here in the hospital bed, I can't help thinking back to the powerful blank surface of those red holiday cups. They represent everything that I despise in this world, and yet somehow I find myself drawn to that beautiful matte finish, the chic, modern plainness of their spotless exterior.

The longer that I dwell on the shape of the new cups, the harder it is to refrain from touching myself, to keep from reaching down between my legs and pumping my fist across my long, hard erection.

I know that I shouldn't be thinking these thoughts, but that's exactly why they are so arousing. The taboo nature of the new cups is exotic and forbidden, seasonally naughty for a hardcore Christian like myself.

I wonder what it would feel like to let me cock slip deep into one of those beautiful red chalices, the warm coffee enveloping my shaft and then covering my balls in its dark, holiday roasted goodness. I can just smell it now, the scent of fresh coffee beans as I get myself off with this handsome beverage.

Suddenly, there is a knock on the door of my hospital room, breaking my concentration. My wife won't be coming by until tomorrow afternoon, and most of my friends have already paid their visits, so I have no idea who this could possibly be.

"Hello?" I call out. "Come on in!"

The door cracks open a bit and then suddenly a handful of massive, red holiday cups come shuffling inside.

I gasp when I see them, completely shocked by the sudden appearance of these incredibly hunky cups.

"What's going on?" I stammer. "What is this?"

One of the cups steps forward, a rugged masculine thing with a sexy white rim and perfectly circular shape. "We heard about your accident, wanted to come by and make sure everything was going okay," the holiday container admits.

"Seriously?" I question. "That's so… sweet."

The cup smiles. "Don't mention it."

I realize now just how incredibly attractive this new cup design is, completely slick and streamlined in a way that truly turns me on. I find myself glancing down at their enormous cocks, which hang down in front of them, at first wondering why these cups are nude and then immediately remember that cups don't wear clothes, obviously.

I'm completely straight, but I'd be lying if I didn't admit I am very impressed with the size of their hulking cup wangs. These shafts are absolutely enormous, and as I watch they begin to slowly grow in size, lifting and extending out towards me.

The lead cup notices, too, glancing around with a smile.

HANDSOME SENTIENT FOOD POUNDS MY BUTT AND TURNS ME GAY

"I'm sorry," he says, "when we came here to make peace I had no idea just how handsome you would be."

"Me either," I admit. "Honestly, I'm not so sure I dislike the new look anymore, it's kind of sleek."

"Thanks," the cup says with a flirtatious smile.

Suddenly, all of that fighting and panicking and arguing just seems utterly silly, a relic of some other me that I barely even know any longer. Who was that angry bearded man yelling into his phone about his Starbutts coffee oppression? Honestly, I have no idea.

"Can I be honest," I finally say.

"Of course," the lead cup says.

"I've always been really turned on by the holiday cups, not in a gay way or anything because I'm totally straight and I know that all cups are dudes," I admit. "I've always been able to keep it under wraps, though, until now."

"I'm listening," the lead holiday cup says, seductively.

"This new design is just so nice, so sensual... so forbidden."

I sit up and throw my legs over the side of the bed, my erotic attraction to these incredible cups blessing me with the power to walk once again for the first time in two days.

I approach the can of holiday beverage containers and suddenly find myself completely surrounded from every side.

"I don't know about this," I whisper, pressing up against one of the cups, "it feels so wrong."

"It's so right, though," he tells me.

Suddenly, my homosexual attraction is just too much to bear. Overwhelmed with lust, I drop down to my knees between them and gaze up with an erotic fire in my eyes.

"Come on," I beg, "I want you guys to show me what the holiday spirit is all about!"

The cups immediately surround me, vying for position as they aggressively push their cocks into my face from every angle.

"Holy shit." I cry out, slightly overwhelmed. I collect myself as best I can and, the next thing I know, I have a beverage container dick in each hand, pumping my tight grip up and down the length of their rock hard shafts. I quickly begin to alternate through the horny coffee vessels, moving from one to the next with incredible efficiency. The beverage containers begin to moan loudly, clearly enjoying the way that I'm servicing them.

"Do you like that?" I ask from down below. "Do you like the way that I beat those thick, gay, non-denominational holiday cocks?"

The red containers in each hand are bucking against my movements, enjoying themselves immensely as I kick the pace of my strokes into double time.

Suddenly overwhelmed with lust, I open my mouth wide and take one of the coffee cups deep down into my throat. I can feel his cock traveling farther and farther within me until suddenly it stops against the limits of my gag reflex. I retch slightly, pulling the cup out of me with a gasp and then wiping the saliva from my lips.

"Let's try that again." I say, looking up at the holiday cup with confidence.

I open wide and take the beverage container deep into my throat again, only this time I'm ready. As the rod drops deeper and deeper I do everything that I can to relax and I suddenly find myself servicing the coffee cup in an expertly performed deep throat.

The beverage container places his red hands on the back of my head and I let him hold me here from a while, clearly enjoying the powerful sensation of filling me with his papery manhood.

Eventually, the gay goblet lets me up and I come away from him with a large gasp, having just enough time to collect myself before suddenly another one of the cups is grabbing me by the head and shoving his cock down my throat, as well.

This container's dick is even larger than the first and he wastes no time between my wet lips, fucking my face in a series of profound and powerful strokes. I reach up and play with his balls while he uses me, then eventually find my way over to two other dicks, which I begin to stroke in tandem with the holiday blowjob.

It's not long until this container passes me off to another coffee cup, and then another, and another until finally all of the seasonal chalices have had a chance at taking me in the mouth. The entire process had gotten me much more excited than I ever expected, and right now there is nothing I want more than for one of these handsome cups to pound my tight gay asshole as hard as he can.

"I want you to fuck me." I suddenly say, pulling the dick out of my mouth and looking up at the gang in a belligerent state of cock drunk lust.

"Slam me full of your promotional holiday spirit!"

I fall forward onto my hands and knees, pulling my hospital gown off and then reaching back to expose my puckered ass to the hunky beverage containers.

Almost immediately, one of the hung cups scoots into position behind me, aligning his girth with my tightness.

"Do it!" I command. "Shove that fat Christmas dick up inside me right now! Show me how gay I really am!"

"You mean fat holiday dick," the cup corrects me.

"That's exactly what I mean!" I scream. "Now do it!"

The cup pushes forward, stretching me to the brink as he slides into my butt. The coffee container lets out a long moan and I quickly join him, the two of us filling the hospital room with our howls of pleasure as he begins to thrust in and out of me with a series of slow and deliberate swoops. I brace myself on the tile floor before me, pushing back against the goblet in perfect harmony with his pumps inward.

"Fuck." I cry out. "That fucking dick feels so good inside of me."

The profanity continues to spill out of my mouth until suddenly one of the beverage containers climbs down in front of me and shoves his massive dick down my throat, cutting me off and rendering my words into a series of strange gargles.

Now pounded from either end, I can feel the warm sensation of prostate orgasm slowly begin to build up from somewhere within me. I reach down and stroke my cock, helping myself along as the sensations build and build until I'm just about ready to explode, when suddenly the cup behind me pulls out and breaks my concentration.

The beverage container gives me a hard slap on the rear and then slides away, allowing another one of the muscular goblets to take his place. Seconds later, this new cup is plowing into me, railing me hard from behind while I moan and groan, my body still trapped between two huge, hard, beverage container dicks.

Eventually, the cups begin to trade places within me just like they did before, each and every one of them taking a turn to plow away at my asshole while my body trembles and shakes with pleasure. The sensation is incredible, a feeling of being both completely used and carnally worshipped. I'm loving every second of it.

"Come." One of the coffee containers orders in his deep, sexy voice.

"I'm trying!" I tell him.

"No, come." The coffee container repeats, pulling me forward so that I'm now straddling his tipped over body. The thick paper cup reaches down and positions his cock at the entrance of my butt, then guides me down slowly onto his length. I close my eyes and bite my lip, impaled completely onto his shaft while the rest of the coffee containers watch and beat themselves off.

The second that this cup is fully inserted I begin to grind against him, riding with a firm pulse that steadily grows faster and faster with every rotation.

"Fuck me! Fuck me!" I'm screaming now, my voice echoing throughout the building, echoing up and down the halls of the busy hospital. "Fuck this tight gay ass!"

One of the other cups has snuck up behind me, and I don't even realize he's there until suddenly I can feel the hard touch of his massive rod against the rim of my already filled back door. I look back at him as a sly smile crawls across my face.

"Two at a time?" I laugh. "Why not? Let's make it a double shot, boys!"

The beverage container whose been knocking at my asshole thrusts forward, successful double stuffing my body and causing me to cry out loud. My fingers dig into the cup below me as I try desperately to adjust to the overwhelming sensation of two cocks deep within.

The sensation is utterly incredible, unlike anything I have ever felt, and it's not long before that same orgasmic seed begins to blossom.

Immediately, I reach down and start to beat my cock, helping myself along. I can feel the prostate orgasm building and building in beautiful waves of pleasure, each one of them expanding farther and farther across my body until suddenly it explodes within me. I throw my head back and scream with guttural intensity, shaking hard as my body struggles to contain all of this beautiful sensation while cum ejects hard from the head of my cock. It feels as though the feeling will never end until suddenly, it simply disappears and I collapse onto the beverage container in front of me.

Moments later, I roll off onto the floor and find myself surrounded by the entire handsome collection of coffee cups. I look up at them with a steady satisfaction in my eyes, watching as they rapidly approach their own powerful orgasms.

HANDSOME SENTIENT FOOD POUNDS MY BUTT AND TURNS ME GAY

"Cover me in your fucking cum." I beg. "Plaster this face with all of your hot holiday loads."

Almost immediately, the coffee containers begin to explode, ejecting their pearly jizz across my manly body as I lie sprawled out on the hospital floor below them. It rains down onto me and covers me from head to toe, creating a thick glaze across my skin by the time they are all entirely finished.

I close my eyes and smile warmly, finally understanding the true meaning of the holiday spirit. It's not about who can spend the most money at the mall, or who can get the most upset by someone saying "Happy Holidays" instead of "Merry Christmas."

No, what the holidays are really about is who can get pounded in the butt by a cup that represents not just one holiday, but every holiday. It's about having an open heart, and an open butt.

TURNED GAY BY THE LIVING ALPHA DINER

When most people think of truck drivers, a very particular kind of guy comes to mind. Large, imposing and bearded are all ways to describe the typical mental image and, as a trucker myself, I can honestly say that that particular imagery is fairly on point. I, however, have my own thing going on.

For a trucker, I'm as young as they come, twenty years old and determined to see a bit of the country before headed off to college where I'll be locked down for years under the weight of text books and tests. Unlike many of my peers, I care about how I look during these long hours on the road, clean-shaven and lean from my push-ups during pit stops.

I'll admit, however, that sometimes it seems my efforts to maintain health and a reasonable appearance are meaningless. The hours out here are lonely and long, and sometimes I'll go days without having a meaningful conversation with anyone other than a gas station attendant. The lack of connection between other human beings makes you disoriented and strange, and eventually you find yourself craving conversation like you would food or water.

On the night that I met Buck, I was starved for interaction. Flying through the open desert of Arizona, it had been hours since I had even seen another pair of headlights slicing through the desert towards me, let alone talked to someone. My girlfriend back home hadn't called in a while thanks to my shoddy phone reception out here, and even if she did I wouldn't have been all that interested in anything Carly had to say. We'd been fighting a lot lately, and to be honest the recent radio silence had been a welcome relief from her constant nagging.

Breaking up with her would be too messy at this point, but deep down inside I have to admit that I know it's just not going to work between us. We're incredibly different in almost every day, and more often that not I find myself sitting across from her at the dinner table just wishing we had something, anything, to talk about. She's a sweet girl, but we're just not meant to be together.

It's been miles since the last town and as the evening sky grows darker my stomach begins to grumble, groaning for my attention like some terrifying desert monster who only emerges to feed at night. The next city is hours away, and the thought of waiting that long for a nice warm dinner makes me nauseous. I normally carry plenty of snacks on hand, but I forgot to stop and grab anything earlier, my mind entirely consumed by the current situation with my distant girlfriend.

Of course, there's not much that I can do about it. Unless by some miracle there is a lone gas station or diner out here somewhere, I'll be waiting until the next town for a late night meal.

Suddenly, as if manifested by some divine power to contradict my negative thoughts, I see a light appear off in the distance.

The closer that I drive, the more I'm able to see what this light is and, moments later, I laugh loudly as the welcoming neon sign of a twenty-four hour diner comes into view. I slap my trucks dashboard playfully, pushing the gas a little harder as I speed across the open highway towards my new destination.

A few minutes later, I arrive at the diner and pull into a designated space for long haul truckers, then hop out of my cab and look up at the neon sign before me.

"Butt House." I read aloud, my eyes scanning across the yellow glowing letters. I notice now that the diner is topped by a large, handsome face, which nods in my direction as we make eye contact.

For some reason, I find myself looking away, slightly taken aback by the restaurants confident demeanor. The guy has swagger, and commands attention to any patrons close enough to get caught in his smoldering gaze. My heart skips a beat and I'm not exactly sure why, but my compulsion for a good meal is much more powerful than any other concern at the moment.

I head across the parking lot, eyes lowered until I reach the restaurants large double doors, crafted beautifully with the buildings impeccable set of abs. Again, I find myself reeling from a mysterious attraction deep down in the pit of my stomach, a sensation that I am vaguely familiar with but previously only in the presence of a beautiful woman.

I'm as straight as they come, but something about this diner immediately has a hold on me, regardless of how desperate I am to deny it. The feeling reminds me of what it was like when I first met Carly, an all-consuming attraction that has since faded from my life. I have felt this sensation a few times, but never once before about a dining establishment.

I reach up and grab the door handle, pulling it open and stepping inside as I try my best to avoid staring too long at the diner's incredible body.

"Hi there, welcome to Butt House!" Says a bubbly waitress as I approach. "Just one?"

"Yeah." I nod, still a little off balance but trying my best to rein it in.

"Right this way!" The waitress says.

The woman leads me through the main hosting area and down a long isle of booths, all of them packed to the brim with hungry eaters. For being so far out in the middle of nowhere, this place boasts an impressively large clientele that includes everyone from fellow truckers to twenty-something couples out on what appears to be a first date.

After seeing what the hot building is working with in here, however, I'm not all that surprised. The place is beautifully lit and breathtakingly clean, decked out in all the trappings of a retro diner but updated with modern flair. The scent wafting my way from somewhere deep in the kitchen is incredible, a savory reminder of the pleasure that's headed my way in the form of delicious food and beverage.

The waitress seats me by one of the windows and then heads off momentarily to bring me a cool glass of water.

I open the menu, perusing my way down the well-balanced selection of various food staples. The selection is incredible, and I'm so impressed that once again I find myself simmering with that familiar, yet confusing, sensation of arousal. I can feel my cock hardening just below the table, aching for release within my pants at the thought of these well crafted burgers and fries. Of course, it's not just the food itself, but the handsome building from which they are served.

Finally, I just can't take it anymore. I have to say something.

"This is a nice place you've got here." I say aloud to the diner, trying my best to seem natural and nonchalant.

"Thanks man." Replies the buildings deep, soothing voice.

The very sound of his words send an erotic chill down my spine and for a moment, I consider leaving right then and there, heading out into the parking lot and calling my girlfriend to confirm my status as a normal, red-blooded, American heterosexual.

Yet, despite my best efforts, I can't will myself into leaving the warm and intoxicating presence of this handsome diner.

"I'm Lars." I finally say, almost stumbling over this simple two-word sentence.

"Turk." Says the diner with a confident swagger in his tone. "Turk Dorby."

"Nice." I say, nodding and trying to keep my cool. "You been out here long?"

"Oh yeah." Says Turk. "I was built about twenty years ago but the remodel happened last summer. Really happy with the way things turned out."

"Me too." I say, trying to sound natural but the words manifesting as awkward and stilted.

Moments later, me and the diner are plunged into silence, my brain desperately searching for something to say as the rest of the patrons chat and clank their dishes around me. "So…" I finally start, not exactly sure where the sentence is headed, just feeling like I somehow need to fill the space between us. My plan backfires however, and with nowhere else to go the word simply hangs there in the air as a reminder of my supreme awkwardness.

Suddenly, the waitress returns, saving me from myself. She sets a tall glass of water in front of me with a pleasant smile. "So, have you decided what you'd like to eat?"

"Oh, yeah." I respond, a little startled. "I think I'll just get a burger."

"Fries?" The waitress asks.

"Sure." I nod.

The woman leaves once again to put in my order, and I immediately find myself alone with the living diner once more.

I'm wracking my brain with what to say next, struggling to find another spark of conversation, when suddenly the building speaks up for himself.

"I saw your truck out front in the parking lot, is this your usual route?" Turk asks.

"Not really." I shake my head. "I took over for a buddy who got sick, my usual drive is pretty far north from here."

"So that's why I've never seen you before." Says the diner. "Glad I did though."

My breath catches in my throat as he says this, immediately picking on an unexpected hint of something more lurking just beneath the surface of his words. "You are?" I ask, my cock literally throbbing to be touched as it aches under the diner table.

"Yeah, I mean, you're a really good looking guy." Turk tells me. "I love it when handsome guys stop in to eat, why wouldn't I?"

"I don't know." I stammer.

"Are you single?" The diner asks.

I freeze, not wanting to answer his very direct, and very important question. I don't want to lie, but my attraction to this living building is just too strong to jeopardize my chances.

"Tonight I am." I finally say.

The diner is silent for a moment, and then finally follows up with, "You gay?"

"Tonight I am." I repeat to him, my voice quaking.

Suddenly, I can feel the bench moving slightly beneath me my ass, just enough to make me jump a bit and look down in surprise.

"How's that?" The restaurant asks.

I relax as much as I can given this is my first homosexual experience, and lay back into the confortable, red leather booth. I let out a long sigh as the seat moves below me, massaging my ass cheeks in a series of powerful, circular movements.

"That feels great." I tell him, trying not to alert the other patrons to the homoerotic encounter unfolding just beneath their noses.

I take one hand and reach slowly down towards my waistline, my rock hard cock craving the tight grip of my fingers. I'm almost there when suddenly my food arrives and I jolt up straight on the bench.

"Here you go." Says the waitress. "Enjoy!"

As soon as the woman walks away I can here the diner's voice drifting over to me in a hushed tone. "Listen, this is a twenty-four hour diner, so it's hard for me to get any alone time... but I want you."

HANDSOME SENTIENT FOOD POUNDS MY BUTT AND TURNS ME GAY

"I want you, too." I confess. "I want you so badly."

"Finish your food and then walk over to that back door, there are stairs leading up to the roof. Go there." Turk explains.

"Okay." I nod.

I dig into my burger but can't seem to find my appetite. Don't get me wrong, the food itself is absolutely delicious, but at this point I'm way to distracted by the illicit invitation from Turk to think of anything else. I'm ready to give myself to him completely, consequences be damned.

I make it halfway through and then finally stand up from my booth in lustful frustration, throwing down more than enough cash to cover the meal.

Immediately, I march through the restaurant and down a small hallway with an inconspicuous door at the end. I open it up and find a flight of stairs waiting for me.

"I don't know if I can do this." I confess, my heart beating a mile a minute. "I lied earlier. I have a girlfriend at home, and I'm straight."

"Then don't do it." The diner says to me, confidently.

I freeze, not knowing what kind of response I expected but finding myself wholly unsatisfied. Maybe that life back home was just a façade, a version of the truth that society demands of me instead of the truth that I want for myself? What if the real me is nothing by a hardcore, gay, diner fucker? I can't help but find the thought of this secret underworld incredibly arousing, the home that I've long been searching for.

"Nevermind." I say. "I'm coming up."

I climb the stairs and push through a door on the top, now finding myself on the roof of the diner with the gorgeous night sky hanging above. Out here in the desert, the stars are more brilliant than I've ever seen then, a true testament to the natural beauty of these southern states.

"Come here." Says Turk, his voice deep, smooth and seductive.

Slowly, I walk across the darkened rooftop until I've reached the other side, where Turks massive face rests imbedded within the front of the building. The sight of him this close is simply breathtaking, a perfect specimen of man that is so attractive I can barely speak, other than to let a sensual whimper escape from between my lips.

"Closer." Turk tells me.

I do as I'm told, moving carefully towards his chiseled face along the edge of the diner.

Up here above the parking lot, its hard not to glance down over the edge, and when I do my heart nearly stops. This building may only be one story tall, but from the looks of it, that is one extra large story.

I also realize now that my perch is not as private as I had hoped, and anyone passing beneath us could easily look up and spot me and the living diner exchanging sweet nothings in the dark.

I'm right up next to the diner's face when he finally tells me to stop. "There."

"What now?" I ask.

"Take out that cock of yours and let me suck you off." Turk commands.

I glance back over my shoulder at the parking lot below. "But, they'll see us."

"I don't care." Turk says. "But if it will make you more comfortable, I'll see what I can do."

Seconds later, the outer building lights begin to lower until they are completely off, leaving me and Turk bathed in nothing but the shining white moonlight.

"Now take out that fat, juicy cock of yours." Repeats Turk, and shove it down my throat.

I slowly unzip my pants and pull out my aching rod, which is hard as can be and ready for action.

Turk smiles and gives me a little wink, then the building opens his mouth and takes me deep into his throat. I let out a long satisfied groan as Turk consumes me, savoring the feelings of his movements as he bobs up and down with his head across my shaft.

"Fuck, that feels so good." I tell him.

Turk continues to service me like this, gaining speed for a moment and them sudden coming to a stop as he takes my cock all the way down into his neck. I plunge way past the giant head's gag reflex and come to rest in his depths, finding myself the lucky subject of a perfectly performed deep throat.

The diner lets me remain here for a while, holding me within him until he finally just can't take it any longer. I pull out and the diner gulps down a frantic gasp of air.

"God damn, I'm so fucking horny for you." Turk tells me. "I need to fuck you right now."

HANDSOME SENTIENT FOOD POUNDS MY BUTT AND TURNS ME GAY

"Then fuck me!" I exclaim with equal desperation.

"Go down into the basement." Instructs Turk. "You'll see my cock jutting out from one of the cement walls. Please, get me off."

I quickly zip up my pants and hurry back towards the rooftop doorway, throwing it open and rushing down the stairs. Immediately, I'm hit with the sweet and savory smells of mouthwatering diner food, but I continue on my way, finding another stairway to goes deeper still into the basement of the building.

Moments later, I'm standing in the middle of an almost completely empty, cement basement, decorated with a few crates of non-perishable foodstuffs and an assortment of tables, chairs and restaurant paraphernalia.

There is one central light hanging down from the center of the room, which illuminates the proceedings in a hard shadowed glow.

"I don't see it." I admit to Turk, scanning the room from his hard dick.

"Back there, behind the boxes." The diner tells me.

I make my way past a few crates of food and suddenly find myself face-to-cock with the buildings massive erect shaft. Turk's dick is beautiful and fully engorged; standing at attention while his two giant balls hang gracefully beneath.

I start by cradling said balls in one hand and slowly stroking his firm shaft with the other, tracing my hand carefully up and down Turk's length.

The building lets out a satisfied and thankful sigh. "Oh yeah, Lars, suck that cock."

"With pleasure." I tell him, then open wide and take him into my mouth. I pump my head up and down his member a few times, making sure to get him nice and lubed up.

I do this for a good while and then remove Turk from my mouth with a mischievous smile. "How about my asshole?"

I turn around and strip off my shirt, followed shortly after my back pants and boxer briefs until I am completely naked. Carefully, I back up towards the wall until the head of Turk's cock is just inches from my asshole. His size is daunting, so I start by testing the edges of my anal limits, pushing back just enough to feel the elasticity of my hole begin to expand around his massive shaft.

Turk enjoys the tease, groaning loudly every time I pull away. Fortunately for him, however, I'm also in no mood to wait. After only a few brief seconds of our anal cat and mouse, I commit fully to the handsome restaurant, pushing down firmly onto his rod and biting my lip as it slides up inside of me.

The way that his enormous size stretches my limits is incredible, a sensation unlike anything I have ever felt. I'd never once taken anything up my asshole, and certainly nothing this large, but as I begin to pump myself up and down across Turk's shaft I start loosen up and let the pleasure overwhelm me. What was once a deep-rooted discomfort has given way to something beautiful and primal, a strange, full sensation that causes my own cock to twitch with every successive slam up my butt.

"Fuck me harder!" I command to the living diner. "Fuck me like the gay little twink that I am deep down inside."

"I thought you had a girlfriend." Turk says, jokingly.

"I'm gay now!" I shout, "You've turned me gay and I love it!"

The restaurant is giving me everything that he's got, slamming my asshole with all of his force as my frantic moans of ecstasy echo throughout the basement.

It's not long before the blossoming gay lust starts to give way to something else. I close my eyes tight, trying to fight the powerful thoughts that begin to seep their way into the dark corners of my unconscious mind. I know that if I accept these ideas my life will completely change, and because of that I make a valiant attempt to hold them off as long as I can.

Still, it's no use. The power of homosexual love is just too strong to be contained.

"Turk." I say, tears of joy beginning to stream down my face as the living building continues to hammer me up the asshole. "I think... I think."

"Don't say it." The diner tells me. "You don't have to."

"I do." I tell him. "I do."

"It's going to change everything if you say it." Turk warns. "Everything."

"That doesn't matter." I gasp through the tears. "I love you."

"I love you, too." Turk admits.

His words hit me like a truck, taking the wind out of my lungs and sending my heart into a spastic fit of lovesick butterflies. I don't even know what to do with myself, but moments later the question is answered as the building begins to shake and tremble around me.

"Oh fuck, I'm gonna cum!" Turk shouts.

"Do it!" I command, pulling his cock out of my asshole and dropping down to my knees in front of him. "Blow your hot white load all over my fucking face!"

The restaurant lets out a few more desperate grunts and then explodes across me with a thick, pearly rope of spunk, which splatters from ear to ear. I smile as the building rains his loads of jizz down onto me, covering me with his cum until completely drained.

When Turk finally finishes I stand up, impressed by his sizable load but desperately horny to cum myself.

"Your turn." Turk says. "Go upstairs and head out back."

I nod and turn to leave, grabbing a spare towel and wiping off my face, then tying it around my waist. Moments later, I emerge once again into the main dining room of the restaurant, where the patrons seem quite confused by the sight of a semi-naked man entering and then exiting their presence.

I waste no time heading out the front door and then making my way around to the back of the restaurant, the night air cool and refreshing against my bare skin.

When I finally make it to the rear of the building and stop to catch my breath.

"Do you see it?" Turk asks.

I scan the restaurant's back wall, trying to understand exactly what my gay lover is getting at until my eyes suddenly come to rest on a beautiful, muscular ass protruding from the brick.

I grin slowly creeps across my face as I step towards Turks beautiful, toned butt, then I pull off my boxer briefs and kneel down behind him, placing my rod at the rim of his puckered hole.

"I want you to slam me until you blow." Turk says. "Fuck me as hard as you can and then shoot that hot load up inside of me."

I push forward, entering the handsome restaurant and immediately falling into a series of rapid thrusts. My hips slap hard against my gay lovers ass cheeks, gaining speed as they go until I am hammering into him with everything that I've got. I can feel the familiar sensation of orgasm welling up inside of me as I continue to slam Turk's tightness.

"Do it!" Turk commands. "Blast that cum into my hot gay restaurant ass!"

The sound of the building's deep, sexy voice puts me over the top and suddenly I am cumming hard, lost in a haze of overwhelming bliss while semen erupts from the head of my cock and spills into my brick and mortar lover. I grasp onto the wall for support as more and more jizz continues to spill out of me.

Eventually, there is nothing left.

I pull out and watch as streaks of my hot pearly load spill forth from Turk's reamed asshole, then I collapse back onto the cement behind me in exhaustion.

"That was incredible." Turk says.

"I love you." I confess to the building, starting to well up again.

This time, however, my tears are different. Instead of joy, I find myself swimming in a sea of fear and apprehension. What happens now?

"I love you, too." Turk says, and then asks with genuine concern, "What's wrong?"

"I want to stay with you." I confess. "I can't just go back to my normal life now."

The building is silent for a moment, deep in thought. "You know, we have a server position opening up." Turk finally says. "You could just stay here and work inside me during the days, then go out with me at night."

"Really?" I ask, sitting upright.

"I mean, if you'd be interested in something like that." Turk offers.

I can't help but smile. "I'd love to stay here and work inside you. Forever."

BIGFOOT SOMMELIER BUTT TASTING

As far as bro's weekends go, a wine tasting is the last thing that I'd be likely to get excited about. Still, it's Jeff's turn to pick and, for whatever reason, nobody else seems to have the same aversion to Napa Valley as I do. If it were up to me, like it was last month, we'd be heading back to Vegas for round two of strippers, gambling and black-out-drunk nights of insane debauchery.

"How much farther?" I ask from the back seat of our SUV, my head pressed hard against the window as I stare out across the passing vineyards that line our drive through the hills. I'll readily admit that the scenery is beautiful, but I'm still not all that excited to spend our whole weekend out here. I'll take beautiful women over beautiful scenery any day.

"This wine better be fucking fantastic." I tell the rest of the car, clearly displaying my disappointment.

I can see Pete glance back at me in the rear view mirror, his expression one of quiet disapproval, but he says nothing.

"You don't like wine country?" Says our friend, Jeff, from the passenger seat. He seems just as put off by my attitude as Pete does but, having picked the location this time around, Jeff has no problem defending his position.

"Dude, they only chicks up here are like eighty years old!" I tell the guys in exasperation.

Pete rolls his eyes. "Alright, fine. You're right, there probably won't be a bunch of chicks up here over the weekend."

"So why are we even going?" I ask, throwing my hands up.

"Because it's not always about chicks, man!" Pete tells me. "We're always out looking for girls, for once can't we just chill as bros and enjoy some wine."

I let out a long sigh. "Sure dude, whatever."

The thing is, Pete's right and deep down I know it. Still, as the number one poon hound in our frat, I've got a reputation to maintain. "I can't wait to get out of this fucking car and get drunk." I say under my breath.

"Well, it looks like you won't have to wait very long." Jeff tells me as we crest over the top a ridge and reveal the beautiful estate of Bilb's Vineyard.

The place is actually pretty impressive, an elegant resort surrounded by acres of beautiful grapes that beckon us onward and up the winding hill.

As we make our ascent we pass by a wealthy looking elderly couple walking down the road.

"Oh my god!" I cry out. "You've gotta be kidding me. We're gonna be the youngest people here by like six decades!"

Pete turns around in his chair. "Nick, chill the fuck out!"

I can tell by his tone that my buddy has finally had enough of my complaining and I back off. I'll keep my mouth shut until he's had a chance to cool down. Who knows, maybe I could find a milf around here somewhere if I put in a little effort.

We soon pull into the main parking area and stop the car, then all three of us climb out and take a good look at our surroundings.

"I'm gonna head in a grab the room keys, you guys feel free to walk around for a bit." Jeff says, taking off for the lobby.

Pete wanders over to the edge of the hill for a moment, checking out some of the vines up close. Meanwhile, I'm already bored out of my skull, so I head towards what appears to be one of the main tasting rooms.

I can see immediately that a small crowd of well-dressed men and women have gathered around a guided, wine tasting tour. They're packed into a room on the side of the estate and the crowd spills out onto the patio, which is where I walk up behind them and find a place to observe.

"And now we have a buttery, oaky wine made right here in our own backyard." Says a deep, soothing voice.

I step forward a little more, trying to catch a glimpse of the speaker who stands before the crowd and then stopping suddenly when I see him, my breath catching in my throat. Right there in front of me is the most beautiful creature I have ever laid eyes on, towering over the others by a good two or three feet. It's bigfoot, covered in fur and sipping leisurely from a glass of deep red wine.

Bigfoot puts the glass down and swallows, clearly enjoying the pleasant taste. "Let's form a line now and you can all come up to try a sip." Bigfoot announces.

The group shifts to one side and forms and orderly queue leading up to bigfoot's table, where the bottle of wine sits. I'm intrigued, and would love to have a taste, but I find myself unable to fall into the queue. I'm completely spellbound by this magnificent beast, frozen in silence as I take in every inch of his incredible features. The monster is more attractive than any human woman, or man for that matter, that I've ever seen, a perfect specimen of pure, animalistic hotness.

Despite my best efforts, and the fact that I'm completely straight as an arrow, I find my cock growing hard within my pants, aching as it stretches against its fabric prison.

"Excuse me… excuse me." I hear a voice coming faintly from behind me, snapping me out of my trance.

I turn around a look down to see a little old woman.

"Are you waiting in line for the wine?" The old woman asks me.

"Oh!" I start, trying to collect my senses. "Yeah, I am. Sorry about that." I take a few steps over and get into the line as it slowly creeps towards this powerful bigfoot sommelier.

My heart is pounding hard in my chest now, pumping gallons upon gallons of anxiety filled blood throughout my body. Only a few more people in line before me until I'll come face to face with the powerful bigfoot. I fix my hair a make sure my shirt is pressed as nicely as I can with my hands.

Finally, it's my turn for a sample of the wine.

"Hello." Says the bigfoot. "How'd you like a taste, sir?"

His imposing presence takes me off guard a bit and I start to stammer, reeling from swagger of this hulking beast. "I… I would love a taste." I tell him.

The bigfoot starts to pour me a glass very slowly and for a moment the entire world seems to stand still, a massive bubble surrounding the two of us in a romantic sphere of attraction. Me and this bigfoot are the only ones who matter right now; me, him and an incredible glass of wine.

"This is our signature Pinot Noir." Says the bigfoot. "Aged fifteen years for a delicious woody finish that I'm sure you'll find very pleasing. This is one of my personal favorite wine's here at Bilb's Vineyard."

As I take the glass from the bigfoot's massive hand our fingers briefly touch, which sends a sharp chill down my spine. For a moment our eyes meet and I find myself overwhelmed by an incredible warm that immediately consumes my soul. I'm not gay, but I want to be with this amazing beast, more than anything I've ever wanted in my life.

"You're gonna have to drink it if you want to taste it." The bigfoot tells me with a wry smile.

I glance down at the glass, snapping out of my brief lover's trance as reality comes flooding back. "Oh… Yeah." I stammer. "Sorry."

I smile coyly as I lift the glass to my lips and take a sip, instantly hit with a powerful, almost sensual, taste. "Oh my god." I murmur.

"Good, right?" Says the bigfoot.

At this point I notice that this majestic creature is watching me just as closely as I've been watching him, his eyes transfixed upon my toned, muscular body as it moves under my tight white shirt. The connection between us is flowing now, moving gracefully back and forth in a strange, unspoken rhythm. A game of cat and mouse played out in subtle movements and looks.

"I'm Torbo Gulgot" The bigfoot suddenly says, extending his hand.

I reach out and give him a firm handshake, barely able to contain my smoldering arousal. "I'm Nick, it's nice to meet you Torbo."

Our hands remain in one another's for slightly longer than you'd expect before Torbo lets go. He takes the glass back and sets it on the counter. "You seem like you have quiet an interest in wine tasting." Torbo observes. "And a great pallet."

I nod. "I hope so."

"Do you have any interest in mixing things up?" Torbo asks, a fierce directness in his expression. "Have you ever considered being the one who is tasted?"

I can't help the confusion that immediately crosses my face. "I'm not sure what you mean."

"Have you ever been…" Torbo let's his deep, sultry voice hang in the air for emphasis. "Tasted?"

"No." I tell him. "I don't think so."

The bigfoot cracks a devilish grin. "Why don't you come back here at eleven tonight and I'll show you?" The creature asks.

"Alright." I confirm nervously. "Sounds good bro."

The beast hesitates and then suddenly everything about his demeanor changes as he straightens up and looks past me at the following person in line. "Next!"

I move out of the way and let the next taster pass, still slightly shaken from my encounter. As the anxiety begins to leave my bloodstream and I begin to stumble back towards my friends, I can't help up look longingly over my shoulder at the mighty bigfoot sommelier. Our eyes meet for a split second, and then he's back to work without another acknowledgement of the moment we just shared.

Out in the parking lot once again, I almost immediately hear the voice of Jeff calling me back over to the car. The guys are all waiting for me with disappointment written all over them.

"Well, it looks like you got your wish." Jeff says, clearly a little upset. "We're going home."

"Why?" I start. "What happened?"

"There was a problem with the rooms." Jeff tells me. "I don't know why, but for some reason the booking didn't go through. We've got no place to stay."

My heart sinks immediately, a freight train of tragic disappointment crushing my soul within seconds of the words leaving Jeff's mouth and hitting my ears.

"But we can't" I stammer. "I need to go to the wine tasting tonight."

"A wine tasting?" Pete cuts in with a wicked smirk. "I thought you wanted to get out of here as soon as possible and find some chicks."

As Pete says this I'm hit with a strange wave of nostalgia, a faint memory of a life that once was. Even though it was just minutes before, my life of chasing women seems like it's an entire decade behind me. Now that I've tasted the succulent flavor of gay bigfoot desire, the thought of anything else, especially human women, seems laughably insufficient.

But of course, the guys aren't going to understand that. How could they?

"I'm over that." Is all that I tell them. "This place is pretty cool, actually."

Jeff just shakes his head. "Well that's good to know, but it's too late now. We don't have a room to stay in. No vacancies."

"None at all?" I ask, getting desperate but trying to hide it. There's no way that I'm missing my private meeting with Torbo tonight.

Jeff eyes me suspiciously, sensing that something is up. "Why do you want to stay so bad now, bro?" He asks.

"You wouldn't understand." I tell Jeff, shaking my head.

"Try me." My friend pushes. "What's up?"

I let out a long sigh. "Have you guys ever met someone who, the second you lay eyes on them, you just know they're gonna mean something important to you."

My friends awkwardly exchange glances with one another.

"Yeah, sure." Jeff offers. "What happened? You already met a girl?"

I shake my head. "No bro... a bigfoot."

Jeff seems confused at first, unsure of what to make of my strange admission. "Like the big monster that lives in the woods?"

"Yeah." I explain. "He's the sommelier here, I just met him. He's giving me a private wine tasting later."

There seems to be a sudden wash of understanding over the gang as they nod slowly, their hearts resonating with the powerful love that I display for Torbo.

"Alright." Jeff says, getting on board. "They don't have enough room for all of us, but there's a single room left if you want to get it for yourself, Nick."

My eyes light up with excitement. "Seriously?"

"Yeah man, it's cool. But you're gonna have to figure out a ride back into town."

Right now a ride back is last thing on my mind, but I appreciate his concern. "It's all good." I tell the gang. "You guys head back, I'll figure it out. I've gotta get ready for my date tonight."

At precisely eleven o' clock I find myself waiting outside the tasting room. What was once an open and inviting place has since been closed up and locked, long white shades drawn across the entirety of the massive, vineyard-facing windows. However, from where I can stand I can clearly make out some movement inside as a shadow crosses the dimly lit room.

I rap gently a few times on the glass and, moments later, the door swings inward, revealing Torbo's handsome, bigfoot face.

"Hello." Torbo says with a smile, stepping back and waving me inside. "Welcome!"

I step into the wine room, trying my best not to act too nervous and failing miserably. "Thanks for having me."

"Let me take your jacket for you." Torbo offers, a perfect gentleman as he removes my suit's blazer from my shoulders.

I've gone full suit and tie for the evening, dressed to impress.

"You look good." Torbo tells me, flat out.

I can't help but blush slightly, my heart skipping a beat at his blatant flirting. I walk over to the same table that Torbo had served me wine at earlier in the day, expecting him to come around the other side and pull out whatever bottle's he got in mind, but instead the giant, hairy bigfoot steps up behind me.

"What is this?" I gasp, my voice filled with anticipation as Torbo's muscular frame envelopes me with its hairy warmth. The answer is obvious, however, and I know it.

"I told you I wanted you to come in for a private tasting." The majestic beast tells me. "I didn't tell you exactly what I wanted to taste though."

"What do you want to taste?" I whimper, my erect cock pressing hard against the fabric of my pants.

"Your ass." Torbo reveals. Without hesitation, he reaches around to the front and unbuttons my belt buckle, undoing it swiftly and then yanking down my slacks.

I let out a startled gasp as Torbo pushes me forward, leaning me over the table in a pose of erotic gay submission. From where I'm positioned now, I can't even manage to look back and see him, but I can feel Torbo's massive, hairy hands moving across my lower body, teasing me relentlessly as my dick aches for release from my boxer briefs.

As if reading my mind, the bigfoot suddenly rips down my underwear as well, unleashing my rock hard dick. More importantly, though, Torbo has exposed my asshole to the open air, and moments later I can feel him pushing his furry face between my ass cheeks.

"Oh my god." I gasp. As a straight man, I've never had anyone explore that region before, and especially not with their tongue. At first, I'm not exactly sure if I like it, but as Torbo continues to lap at my puckered asshole, I find myself loosening up and enjoying the ride. Soon enough, I'm overwhelmed by arousal and can't help reaching back to grab my ass cheeks with both hands, spreading myself wide so that Torbo can feast blissfully on my human butt.

"That feels so fucking good." I moan, reeling from the sensation.

Torbo pulls back for a moment. "It tastes good, too. The creature tells me. There is a definite high note of rose, with some smooth, buttery lows and a fine nutty finish. This is a delicious asshole."

"Thank you." I tell him, my words cutting off abruptly as Torbo dives back in and causes my breath to catch in my throat. "God damn, that feels so good."

Just when I think that my pleasure can't be elevated to an even higher plateau, my bigfoot lover does exactly that, reaching between my legs and grabbing ahold of my thick rod with his massive bigfoot paw. The creature begins to pump his firm grip up and down my length as he eats my asshole, causing my body to spasm and quake in all kinds of unfamiliar ways.

"Oh fuck." I start to murmur over and over again. "Oh fuck, oh fuck."

The intense pleasure loosens my grip on space and time, setting my mind adrift in a sea of unquantifiable sexual bliss. I feel like I've been standing here forever with this bigfoot's face buried in my ass, when suddenly Torbo pulls back and spins me around.

The powerful beast stands and hoists me up onto the table, spreading my legs and then gracefully swallowing my rod into his warm bigfoot mouth. He takes me deep, expertly relaxing his already massive throat as his black lips reach the base of my rod. The monster holds there for a moment, letting me thoroughly enjoy the sensation of his depths before letting me up and allowing me a large gulp of air. The next thing I know, he's back at it, only now Torbo gets to work pumping his huge bigfoot head over the length of my shaft like a beastly jackhammer.

"Fuck, that feels so good." I moan, moving my hips to the rhythm of Torbo's mouth. I'm ready to blow now, but as much as I enjoy the way Torbo is servicing me, I crave nothing more in the world than to taste his huge bigfoot dick for myself.

After a moment, I push Torbo back and slip off of the table, climbing down onto the ground in front of him.

"Do you think I could suck on that fat cock of yours?" I beg, submitting myself to this beautiful bigfoot wine expert. "I'd love a taste for myself."

Torbo obliges, unzipping his pants and pulling out the biggest dick I've ever seen; long, hairy and standing at full attention. He places his member so that it rests gently against my puckered lips, letting me kiss the head of his shaft and then lick him from balls to tip. After admiring Torbo's phallic beauty for a while, I just can't take waiting any longer and swallow his dick hungrily.

Torbo let's out a deep sigh as I take him down as far as I can, stopping only when his length reaches my gag reflex and I retch slightly, unprepared for his incredible size. I come up and take in a frantic gasp of air, trying to relax in the face of the creature's daunting manhood.

"Too much to take for a straight boy?" Torbo laughs.

I shake my head. "I've got this, bro."

Immediately, I take Torbo between my lips for a second attempt, pushing down farther and farther until he slides confidently past my gag reflex in a beautifully performed deep throat.

The chiseled creature has removed his shirt, and I look up at the once mythical beast admiringly, taking in his incredible body from my viewpoint down below. Torbo places his hands on the back of my head and starts to pump me up and down, guiding my lips across his length as he fucks my handsome face.

The beast is somehow powerful and gentle with my body at the same time, careful not to hurt me but definitely enjoying his display of power while he uses me like a gay human play toy. Torbo moves me slowly at first, taking long deep thrusts into my throat as he groans happily, then begins to speed up within me until eventually he's slamming his cock into my mouth with rapid brutality. I'm loving every seconds of it.

As Torbo continues to have his way with me, I reach down between my legs and get to work beating off my cock. My stomach clenches tight as I move myself along, the chills bubbling farther and farther across my body until eventually I find myself hovering near the realm of a powerful orgasm. I start to moan into the dick that plugs my mouth, the sound vibrating through Torbo's dark flesh until suddenly, the beast pulls himself out and hoists me up next to him.

Torbo knows exactly what he wants and he moves with confidence, spinning me around with a single rough tug and then pushing me up against one of the wine racks. He saddles up behind me with his massive, muscular body, aligning his cock with the entrance of my untouched, previously straight asshole.

"Do it!" I scream. "Shove that giant bigfoot dick into my tight little brohole!"

Torbo doesn't have to be told twice, immediately trusting forward and stretching the limits of my puckered butt. I can feel myself expand around the girth of his cock, my insides stretching to the brink as his throbbing bigfoot shaft slides deeper and deeper within my ass. I brace myself against the rack before me, but can't help looking back to watch Torbo's enormous bigfoot snake slides up inside.

When Torbo finally reaches the hilt I let out a long satisfied string of expletives, trying desperately to find the words for this incredible sensation that fills my ripped body. I can't, so Torbo helps me.

"Tell me you like that big, fat bigfoot sommelier cock." The creature commands with his deep voice.

"I love that bigfoot sommelier cock!" I tell him, my words trembling as the movements of his dick begin to slowly speed up.

"You're a bad bay aren't you?" Torbo demands to know.

"I'm so bad." I tell him, my eyes rolling back into my head. "I shouldn't love fucking this big bigfoot dick so much; but I do, I really do."

Torbo slaps my toned ass hard, sending a shiver of excitement down my spine. He's railing into me frantically now, pumping in and out with all of his muscular force while I hang onto the wine rack for dear life.

I can't believe that this incredible beast is really fucking me, taking pleasure in my body as we share a moment of mutual carnal bliss. I've submitted myself to him completely, and yet somehow I feel free; free to explore sex the way that I'd like to do if there was no shame or guilt associated with our desires.

"Harder!" I scream at Torbo. "Turn me gay!"

He's going as fast as he can, but I want more. I want him to absolutely pummel my asshole, to fuck me harder than I've ever been fucked before, leaving my legs wobbly and my eyes wet with lustful gay tears.

"Harder!" I demand again. "Fuck me like the dirty gaybro that I am!"

Torbo suddenly grabs me from the rack and spins me around, lifting me back up onto the table once more. He grabs my legs and lifts them back so that they rest against either one of his hulking, muscular shoulders and then aligns his cock with the already reamed entrance of my asshole.

"You want it hard, huh?" Torbo asks. "Let's see how you handle this."

"Shove it in!" I command. "Slam my bro ass with that thick fucking cock!"

Inspired by my verbal motivation, Torbo pushes deep into my butt, which expands wide to accommodate the girth of the monster's huge member.

"Holy shit!" I cry out, my hands gripping the edge of the table tightly. "My tasty bro ass!"

Torbo is pulsing in and out of me with slow, deliberate movements, my legs spread wide by his huge, muscular arms.

"You're fucking me so good." I tell him. "Let's blow our loads together, bigfoot bro."

Torbo nods in agreement, and I reach down to my rock hard cock. I begin to pleasure myself again with one hand as Torbo pumps faster and faster into my tight asshole, his thrusts gaining speed until he is railing my butt with everything that he's got. My legs bounce in the air on either side of the powerful monster.

"I'm almost there!" I cry out.

"Me too, me too." Torbo tells me, not letting up for even a second.

"I'm so close!" I moan.

Suddenly, it hits me like a freight train. My entire body seizes up and I clench forward, then seconds later everything explodes with orgasmic pleasure, throwing my head back off of the edge of the table. I arch up and cry out with a powerful yell, my body barely able to contain all of the incredible sensations that flow through it. "Fuck!" I shout as jizz blasts from the head of my shaft.

Torbo immediately plows forward and holds deep within me, letting out an anguished cry of his own. I can feel his load eject hard inside of my rear, pumping my asshole full of his thick, milky spunk as the beast's eyes remain tightly shut, his teeth gritted.

"Fuck!" Torbo groans, the eruptions of jizz still flowing until finally there's just not enough room within my asshole and then semen comes spurting out of the sides. It runs in streaks down from the edges of my plugged hole, cutting thick streams of white down the curve of my toned ass and onto the table below.

Finally, Torbo falls back, panting with exhaustion. A satisfied smile slowly creeps across his devilishly handsome face. "Now that was satisfying." Torbo tells me.

The next time that I see the guys a year has passed. Me and Torbo have started a vineyard of our own and are living peacefully in the countryside, far away from the hectic buzz of the big city.

I can hear the gangs loud, thundering bass as my friends pull up the front gravel drive, and I come out to greet them with open arms. It's been a while, and I can't wait to share my now life with them.

"Whoa, this is amazing." Pete tells me, giving me a warm hug and then pulling back to look me up and down. "You look good dude, you been working out?"

I nod. "Yeah, me and Torbo run through the hills every morning, it's kind of our thing."

"This is beautiful." Jeff interjects. "Thanks so much for having us up here for a guys weekend."

"Absolutely." I tell them.

"I feel like it was just yesterday that you were complaining about going to a wine tasting... and now you're having us out here for one." Jeff laughs. "So crazy."

A smile slowly crosses my face. "Oh no, it's not a wine tasting." I tell them.

"It's not?" Jeff asks. The guys exchange confused glances.

"It's a tasting." I clarify. "Just not wine."

"I don't get it." Pete admits. "What's going on here?"

I laugh and take Pete's bag out of his hand, then turn and start heading for the house. "You'll see." I tell the gang. "But first there's a nice group of bigfeet that I'd like you to meet, Torbo's friends from the deep woods. You're gonna love them."

"Oh yeah?" Jeff asks. "Why is that?"

"Because they've got great taste." I tell him.

SLAMMED IN THE BUTT BY THE LIVING LEFTOVER CHOCOLATE CHIP COOKIES FROM MY KITCHEN CABINET

Like it or not, the hours you work will have a huge impact on the rest of your life. Not just the hours themselves, but when and where they occur.

We like to think that we're defined by what's inside, and most of the time this is the case, but when you spend as much time behind the bar as I do it also starts to change you in unexpected ways.

First of all, I can't even remember the last time I saw any of my daytime friends, the ones who work away at their nine-to-fives while the sun hangs overhead and blesses them with all of those good vibes and Vitamin-D. These are the ones who can grab dinner after work at pretty much any restaurant they want, without stooping to the level of whatever fast food is still open while I'm driving home, desperately trying to make it into bed by the time the sun starts creeping up over the distant horizon.

The bizarre schedule kinda makes me feel like a vampire, which is cool I suppose, but I also miss all of my friends.

Sure, every once in a while they'll stop by and grab a quick drink of milk, but when I'm on the clock I don't have much time to chat, especially in a milk bar as crowded as this one. I can barely get in a hug and make a bit of small talk, but the second this is over then it's back to the grind, mixing up strawberry Quick and popping the caps off of ice cold chocolate milk in the glass bottle.

Unless it's a Sunday night, of course, but who wants to go out on a Sunday.

The second way working as a bartender changes you is that it builds your tolerance for slow, stupid, or otherwise annoying people. There is more anger and vileness directed at me while I'm serving milk than I could have ever imagined, and somehow I've learned to deal with it.

People hopped up on ice cold milk are already a little frustrating, but when they don't feel like they're getting served fast enough, or when they simply want to start a fight, things quickly get amplified.

Fortunately, I have a whole slew of bouncers ready to pounce at a seconds notice, grabbing the offending patron by the neck and literally throwing them out to the curb on more than one occasion. Fortunately, most of the indiscretions of these folks aren't quite bad enough for a forced removal, they're just rude.

This is where the changes come in. Over the first few weeks I felt like I was more short tempered than usual, but eventually all of that anger just stopped. I became thick-skinned, impervious to any bad behavior that might have otherwise bummed me out for days. Now when I call on the bouncers to kick someone out, I do it with a smile and a nod.

It sounds nice, and I guess it's better than losing my mind every couple of nights, but once that wall has been built up it's a very, very difficult thing to tear down. I feel the emotion that I once experienced drifting away, all of the anger and frustration and rage, but all of the excitement and joy, as well.

Or maybe I'm just taking all of this a bit too seriously.

Regardless, here I am again, standing behind the bar and staring out mindlessly as my head swirls with thoughts about how I ended up here and what kind of havoc it's wreaking on my life. The voice of the man standing before me finally stamps me out of it.

"Hey, hey!" he shouts, waving.

I glance down at him, realizing now that I must have been zoning out for quite a while.

"Can I get a drink?" he asks.

I nod, quickly collecting myself.

"Just a two percent glass of the white stuff," the guy orders, clearly a little annoyed but also not the biggest jerk I've ever encountered around here. Not by a long short.

After all, he has a point. Right now I'm on the clock; the introspection can wait. "Sorry about that," I say, and then quickly get to work fixing his drink.

HANDSOME SENTIENT FOOD POUNDS MY BUTT AND TURNS ME GAY

It's Sunday night, so fortunately things are slow enough that I can actually get away with a little bit of relaxation on the job. However, that also means there's nobody else here to help me or to give me a quick nudge when I turn into a complete weirdo and stare off into space.

I finish up and hand off the man's drink. "That'll be thirteen bucks," I inform him.

The guy pulls out his wallet and gives me a twenty, then takes his glass of two percent and walks off to meet his group of friends in the corner booth. That's a hell of a tip for a bartender that barely even knew he was there.

I suppose this is one of the few advantages of my job. When you're as handsome as I am, it's hard not to make a killing in tips even when you're having an off night. Thanks to my big bright eyes and boyish good looks, I could have given the guy a shot of hot chocolate and he still would have been just as generous. I'm the type of guy that these New York hipsters fall all over themselves for; a few tattoos, cutting edge style, but enough good genes to have muscular, toned body to back it all up.

But now I'm drifting off again, overthinking everything as the internal dialog of my own brain spins out of control.

I look around the place, realizing now that they are basically the only ones in here and letting out a sigh of relief. I'm in too weird of a mood right now to deal with any more customers that aren't the regular's I've come to know and love.

Suddenly, I notice movement across the bar, the door swinging open and a group of tall, perfectly round disks entering through the darkness. I don't have to see their faces to know exactly who it is, the familiar walk of my chocolate chip cookies immediately registering within the deepest recesses of my brain.

A smile quickly crosses my face as the gang of them approaches, all five of the desserts stepping into the light as they make their way up to the bar.

I can't help doing an excited dance as I make my way around the counter and hug Gorbot, who has always been my favorite of the bunch.

"Oh my god, what are you guys doing here?" I ask. "Shouldn't you be sitting in my kitchen cabinet?"

"We just thought we'd stop in and say hi," Gorbot says with a smile.

"It's been a while," my living cookie Shipple adds, "you stopped eating us last month and now I feel like we never see you."

I roll my eyes. "I'm on a diet, you know this."

"Well, we figured we would come to you instead," Gorbot continues.

I shake my head, not knowing what to say and suddenly finding myself incredibly touched by the food's love and support. I've only had these cookies in my cabinet for five or six weeks now, but I have never felt anything but love for this collection of awesome deserts.

Of course, I'll admit that there are times when I realize this feeling of love may be a little more sexually potent than I'd like to admit, but that kind of goes without saying when you consider the fact that we're all pretty attractive and living in a post-college world where casual sex and hook ups with your own living food is the norm. In reality, these cookies are completely off limits, there to eat and nothing more, but I'd be lying if I didn't admit that my mind had wandered there once or twice.

I honestly think the thing that's most attractive about my five living cookies has nothing to do with their handsome chocolate chip features; however, it's the fact that they seem a little competitive for my attention and approval. Of course, Gorbot usually wins, but the quarreling will always be so exciting to watch.

"You guys want something to drink?" I ask, continuing to pass out hugs left and right before finally returning to my position behind the bar once more.

"Just a round of milks," Gorbot informs me.

I smile and fetch a few bottles for them, popping off the tops and then passing them out.

"How much?" my living cookie asks.

I laugh. "Please, these are on the house tonight."

"You sure, Nick?" Shipple chimes in. "Your boss isn't going to get mad?" He nods up towards a security camera behind me, the menacing little box and it's blinking red light pointed directly at us.

I smile and then lean in close to the crew of living cookies. "Top secret info. It's fake."

"Whoa, really?" Gorbot laughs.

I nod.

"Well alright then," my living cookie says, hoisting his milk into the air. "Let's party then!"

The desserts all cheer and for a brief moment I actually *feel* something,

HANDSOME SENTIENT FOOD POUNDS MY BUTT AND TURNS ME GAY

a wave of joy and humanity washing across me in a soothing pulse. I had no idea what a welcome break this surge of emotion would be until it comes.

Suddenly, however, I'm pulled back down to reality as I notice the guy that I had previously helped is standing behind my living cookies, angrily trying to push past and make his way up to the bar.

"Hey, what's up?" I question, putting up my wall again as the man arrives and set his glass down angrily.

"This two percent tastes like skim," the man states bluntly.

Immediately, my living cookies go quiet, observing the situation with the intensity of disciplined guard dogs, just waiting for their chance to pounce.

I glance at Gorbot, signally to him that everything is okay.

"Can I make you a new one?" I ask the man who had seemed so generous when he tipped me before.

"I don't know, can you?" the man asks, a decidedly juvenile comeback. Obviously, this guy has had a little too much milk tonight and is simply looking to start a fight, but I still remain perfectly calm. I am made of stone, and nothing can penetrate my cool exterior.

"I sure can," I tell him, with a smile that comes across as genuine as it possibly can.

In most situations, this would be the end of it, but tonight this particular asshole is looking for conflict and he's not backing down until he gets it. The man raises his glass up in the air and then turns it over, pouring the drink out across the bar as I jump back in surprise.

Immediately, my living cookies are upon him, Gorbot laying the guy out in a single punch while the others grab his crumpled body and begin to carry him towards the door. This would have worked out just fine had the gentleman in question not been accompanied by a booth full of other angry loudmouths who quickly come to his aid. The next thing I know, all hell has broken lose, the entire bar now a tumbling fistfight between man and food. I glance over and see Rick, the bouncer, running across the room and diving into the fray, pulling people apart and trying his best to deescalate the situation.

"Them!" I yell to Rick, pointing at the group of angry patrons. "Get them out of here!"

The bouncer nods and, somehow, manages to separate the groups enough so that the fighting stops momentarily.

CHUCK TINGLE

"All of you," Rick yells, a fire in his eyes as he points to the asshole and his buddies, "get the fuck out of here and don't you dare come back."

I can see now that the men are completely bruised and beaten, clearly not fairing well against my muscular living cookies who all seem to be perfectly fine, not the least bit crumbly after this unexpected battle.

I have to admit, for as violent as this brutish display was, there is something kind of hot about the way that my living cookies all rushed in to defend me. I don't *want* to be proud of them, especially after they threw the first punch, but I am. Maybe it's the fact that my emotions have been kept so pent up inside lately, or maybe this is just a feeling that his been bubbling up within me for a while. Whatever the reason, I can't help feeling the slightest bit aroused by the rough and tumble deserts.

I know, I know, these are my living cookie's we're talking about here and there is absolutely no way that anything could ever happen between us. The hint of desire that is sparking within me is not something I would ever act on, but it feels so good to nurse and feed this little flame. After all, it's just a fantasy, right? It's not like we are actually ever going to hook up, especially since there are five of them left in the package and only one of me.

Still, I'll let them be my knights in shining armor for a brief moment.

Eventually, Rick convinces the angry patrons to leave, closing and locking the door behind them.

"Let's shut it down," Rick says, "it's late and I don't have the patience to deal with anymore dicks like that. I don't want you to have to wait around for customers that never come, either."

I nod. Typically, a bouncer would be the last guy to make this kind of call, but he's close friends with the owner and I trust his judgment on this slow Sunday eve. Looks like nobody is that interested in drinking milk tonight.

"Fair enough," I tell him. "I've just gotta clean up and let my living cookies finish their drinks."

Rick glances over at the guys curiously. "Ah ha! I've heard a lot about you. Nick's had you in his cupboard for a while now, right? I hear you taste great," he says, shaking everyone's hand. "I thought you guys were just some random heroes for a minute there."

"Oh, they're heroes," I offer.

Eventually, Rick leaves and the whole gang of us finds ourselves with our own private bar for the night.

We chat and catch up, enjoying each other's company over on a collection of vintage leather couches in the back corner. The desserts even talk me into having a glass of skim for myself, which is pretty nice and makes me loosen up a bit more.

My life has just gotten so tense lately, and the relief that I feel sitting around with these handsome gay confectioneries is almost indescribable. I don't even fight it when my thoughts begin to drift into the places where they shouldn't, noticing how toned and muscular Shipple's chips have gotten, or sitting a little too close to Gorbot and placing my hand on his crumbling, baked edge.

The rest of my living cookies notice this but say nothing, clearly trying to play it off as a little harmless fun like I am. I can't help but feel that we all sense it, however, the strange tension that has infiltrated our collective. Maybe it's the milk, or the pulsing adrenalin left over from the fight earlier. Whatever the cause, it's potent.

"I'm so glad you all came to see me," I tell Gorbot, gushing. "I really am. I mean, I just spend so much time in this place feeling nothing at all, surrounded by people but closed off to everyone. I feel like I can totally open up to you guys."

"Of course you can open up to us," Gorbot says, pulling me even closer to him, "we're your cookies."

My heart skips a beat as our warmth mingles, the familiar scent of his sugary body wafting into my nostrils.

"I feel like I can tell you anything," I finally admit, the words somehow taking on much more weight than I ever expected them to. They seem to hang in the air before us, waiting patiently to be taken advantage of.

"Like what?" Shipple finally asks, pulling the trigger. "Something on your mind, Nick?"

I shake my head, but can't help revealing myself with a mischievous smile that creeps out across my face despite my best efforts to contain it. "No, just saying," I tell them.

Shipple eyes me suspiciously. "I've seen you devour enough of my friends to know when you're full of it," he explains. "Come on, you can tell us. What's on your mind?"

I bite my lip, as if it could somehow keep my mouth from opening up and spilling the beans, but my efforts are useless.

"Okay," I finally say, "but you have to promise that you won't think it's weird."

My living cookies all nod, every one of them locked onto me with rapt attention.

"I thought it was really sexy the way that you cookies all defended me," I finally admit.

The desserts all crack wide smiles, exchanging glances with one another.

Shipple shrugs and chuckles to himself. "That's your big secret, Nick? Do you realize how sexy I think you are *all* the time?"

My breath catches in my throat as I try to remain composed. I don't want any of them to know how horny this revelation makes me. Like I said before, I'm typically pretty great with my poker face, but in this case I've let myself slip. It's almost as though I want to be caught.

I realize now just how badly I want to feel something, to let any emotions surge through me the way that they used to before I took on this stupid job. I want to be free to make crazy impulsive decisions, I want to be the one getting into trouble inside of breaking the trouble up.

"It's too bad you're my living cookies," I finally say, my voice trembling slightly. "You know, food and nothing more."

"Why?" asks Gorbot, turning his brown cookie head to look down at me. I can feel his thumb running back and forth across the flesh of my hip, testing my limits.

"Because we could all hook up if you weren't on my grocery list," I tell him, diving in completely.

The cookies are silent, the entire gang of us as tense as we've ever been. Music plays softly over the speakers above, doing it's best to fill in the awkward empty space while my heart nearly pounds out of my chest.

Suddenly, Gorbot leans in and kisses me deeply on the mouth.

My first instinct is to pull away, but as the surge of relief washes over me I switch gears completely. The floodgates have been opened and there is no going back. I am fully invested in this gay fantasy now, and I intend to take things all the way. Even though I am perfectly straight, I'm determined to get the homoerotic sensation that I so desperately crave from my dessert.

Suddenly overwhelmed with lust, I stand up from the leather couch,

HANDSOME SENTIENT FOOD POUNDS MY BUTT AND TURNS ME GAY

letting the guys watch me like a pack of hungry animals while I stroll out into the middle of them.

"If we're gonna do this," I say, "let's fucking do it. Now stand up and get out those cocks of yours."

Then cookies don't have to be told twice, rising from their chairs in the circle and then quickly pulling out their massive, engorged shafts. I drop down into a squat between them, admiring their impressive members as they surround me in a forest of sugary, living cookie dick.

Overwhelmed with gay arousal, begin to furiously suck them off, pumping my head up and down over the length of their rods as I make my way around the circle. It appears that the desserts weren't expecting such adept oral skill from their horny owner, but they quickly fall into step with my passionate blowjobs, placing large, familiar hands on the back of my head and helping to pump me up and down.

Eventually, I take one of my living cookie's giant rods and push it down as far as I can, letting his length slide deep into the depths of my throat. Despite my enthusiasm, however, I'm not quite ready for Shipple's incredible size and, the next thing I know, I'm gagging on his mammoth baked dick.

The handsome confectionery pulls out as I sputter and gasp, trying desperately to collect my senses. "I'm sorry, let's try that again," I offer.

I open wide and my living cookie slips his cock within for a second time, only now I've somehow managed to relax enough to allow his manhood to be fully consumed. His cock sinks deeper and deeper into my throat, finally coming to rest with his balls pressed tightly against my chin.

I look up at Shipple's chocolaty eyes and give a playful wink, allowing him to enjoy the sensation of complete consumption as he holds me here.

Meanwhile, I reach out with each hand and grab ahold of two other massive living cookie dicks, stroking them off in a series of slow, firm pumps. The desserts seem to enjoy this greatly, letting out a chorus of deep moans as they trade positions within my hands.

Eventually, I run out of air and am finally forced to pull back with a gasp, releasing Shipple's huge rod from my throat. I am so horny that I can hardly stand it, trembling with anticipation as I look up at the gang with wild, lustful eyes.

"I can't believe this is happening," I tell them, "I can't believe I'm sucking off the leftover cookies from my kitchen cabinet."

"Trust me, I can't believe it either," Shipple admits.

"I want you inside of me," I beg. "I need your big, sweet, cocks."

I stand up and walk over to a nearby coffee table, stripping my clothes off as I go and then bending my toned, muscular body over it. I look back at the forbidden men coyly.

"Get over here and pound this tight gay ass!" I command.

My handsome living cookies immediately follow my instructions and, the next thing I know, they have surrounded me once more, beating off their dicks while they watch Gorbot align his cock with my puckered butthole. I can feel him teasing the edges of my tightness, then moments later he slides deep inside of me.

I let out a sharp yelp as my body adjusts to my living cookie's massive size. He is absolutely enormous, the thickness of his taboo shaft stretching my limits and filling me completely.

My muscular living cookie pumps in and out, slowly at first and then gaining speed with every thrust until, eventually, he is pounding me with everything that he's got. The force of his confident slams shakes the coffee table below me, our loud rhythm ringing out through the whole bar.

"Oh fuck, oh fuck," I begin to cry, unable to contain all of the pleasant prostate sensation as it flows through me. "You're fucking me so good!"

I'm ready to continue my erotic diatribe but, at this point, another one of my living cookies kneels down before me and shoves his massive rod between my lips. Suddenly, I find myself completely silenced, unable to make any sound other than a wild grunt as I'm pounded from either end.

These cookies slam away at me brutally but, surprisingly, the more rough they are with my body, the more it turns me on. I want to be completely used by my living desserts, their own personal sex toy for the evening.

Eventually, the confectionaries in both of my holes pull out and let another pair have a turn, trading places within my tightness as they form lines at either end of the coffee table. Each living cookie is just as skilled as the first, however, picking up right where the last one left off and plowing away at my butt with a passionate fury.

I can feel the first hints of prostate orgasm begin to blossom within me, starting deep down in my stomach and then spreading out as it courses across my arms and legs. I start to tremble and shake, my muscles spasming while I reach a single hand down to stroke my cock.

Closer and closer I edge towards a powerful orgasm, almost reaching the final breaking point when suddenly my living cookie pulls out of me and give my ass a hard slap.

I look back at him, confused. "What's going on?" I ask.

"There's something we've all joked about doing for a while," my living cookie admits. "I think now is the time."

"What do you mean?" I question, not quite sure what to make of his erotic admission.

The handsome desserts don't answer, but two of them silently help me to my feet while I am replaced on the coffee table by one of my living cookies. The familiar food is laying on his back, his massive cock jutting out from his ripped body like a beautiful tower of aching flesh.

"Get on," he commands.

I do as I'm told, throwing my muscular legs around either side of the table and then crouching down onto the massive dick below me. As my living cookie enters my reamed out butthole I grab onto his shoulders, guiding my descent until I am completely impaled across the length of his giant member.

It feels absolutely incredible, and my body instinctively begins to buck against him in slow but firm swoops. Every grind of my hips grows harder and deeper, my body still trying to adjust to his size until finally the sensation is just too incredible and I begin to fuck him hard, riding his dick like a jackhammer.

"Fuck yes!" I scream, the sensation of orgasm boiling up within me once more. "Oh my god, that dick is so fucking good! Fuck me! Fuck me hard!"

I'm so caught up in the moment that I barely notice a second muscular dessert climb into position behind me. Suddenly, all of that changes however, as this leftover cookie places his thick cock against the puckered entrance of my already filled asshole and slams forward, double penetrating me ruthlessly.

I let out a wild scream of pain and pleasure, my body barely having any time to adjust to the powerful fullness. I look back at my living cookie in shock, but what started as a moment of anger quickly transforms into a lustful snarl. The feeling is unexpected, unlike anything I have ever experienced, but it's also quite amazing.

Soon enough, I find myself fully enjoying the sensation of their double plugging. The three of us eventually find a rhythm together, pulsing like some strange, sexual hybrid. My breathing heavy, I reach down between my legs and begin to frantically beat my dick, adding even more pleasure to the already overwhelming onslaught. My eyes roll back into my head as a long, powerful groan escapes my throat.

"I'm gonna cum," I start chanting, "I'm gonna cum, I'm gonna cum, I'm gonna fucking cum so hard!"

The tension within me has built to a breaking point, ready to burst as I tremble and shake wildly. Everything in my body is clenched tight, just waiting to explode until finally it does and I let out a roar of joyful ecstasy.

"I'm cumming!" I scream, my jizz flying everywhere.

The living cookies who are double fucking my butthole don't let up for a second, giving it to me with everything that they've got and sticking with it throughout the entire orgasm. Every slam within me just adds to the blinding throbs of sensation, treating me to wave after wave of bliss until, finally, I fall forward in exhaustion. I am completely spent as I lay here against the food.

"That was fucking amazing," I gush.

These handsome desserts aren't finished with me yet, though.

The next thing I know, the living cookie who fucks my asshole from behind has picked up speed, slamming me hard and then pushing deep as he explodes with a payload of hot chocolate syrup. His warm sweetness fills my ass quickly, gushing forth with a supernatural intensity until its squirting out from the edges of my packed anal rim.

"Fuck yeah, shoot that chocolate syrup deep into your owner's maxed out asshole," I encourage. "Fill me up!"

When my living cookie finally pulls out a whole torrent of chocolate comes with him, the liquid running down my ass and providing ample lube for the next living confectionery in line.

Soon enough, another edible lover has stepped up to take the last one's place, aligning the head of his shaft with my rim and then plowing forward in a second, brutal double anal penetration. My toned living cookie quickly gets to work slamming my butthole, enjoying my tightness and then thrusting deep to release a load of his own.

"Oh shit!" I cry out, my handsome lover's syrup swirling within me as it mixes with the sticky sweetness that came before it.

My living cookie stays put until he has completely emptied himself and then finally pulls out to allow a third one to take his place.

The guys continue like this for what seems like forever, plowing my reamed butthole and then eventually blowing their load into the mix with the others. Eventually, the last living cookie finishes within me and I find myself with only one left to satisfy, Gorbot, who has been so diligently ramming my ass from the front.

Gorbot pushes me off of him and then stands up, beating off his dick furiously while I look up and smile from my knees below. I stick out my tongue, coaxing him onward until finally my living cookie explodes across my face. His warm, brown spunk flies everywhere, though I manage to catch quite a bit of it in my mouth and then swallow hungrily.

"That was really nice," I tell Gorbot, "you taste great."

Gorbot reaches down and takes me by the hand, helping me to my feet. "Of course, I do, I'm four hundred calories of nothing but fat and sugar."

I glance around the circle of handsome gay desserts, the guys looking beautifully toned and muscular as they catch their breath in the dim light of the bar.

"We can't tell anyone," I remind my living cookies. "I don't want to have to fuck everything in the entire kitchen."

"Of course not," Gorbot assures me. "Never again."

I think about this for a moment and then suddenly shake my head. "On second thought, tell everyone you can. I can't want to see what a living cheeseburger feels like pounding away at my butt."

The cookies all burst into a fit of laugher and we all exchange enthusiastic high fives.

SHARED BY THE CHOCOLATE MILK COWBOYS

Out here in the west we have our own rules, and these rules are young. In fact, some of them are still being written day by day as folks continue to expand into the wild frontier from their posh city life on the East coast. Whether by wagon or train, they're coming, and with them comes a whole new era of life in this great country that is America.

Their arrival is bittersweet, however.

When they finally get here, what will they know of the work that was spent turning this landscape from the wild, wild west into a civilized place to dwell? Eventually, those who come out to these deserts will find convenience at every turn and think nothing of it, assuming that it was always this way. They will have no idea the blood sweat and tears that feel into the very dirt that they walk upon, no concept of the toils and tribulations of generations past.

The heroes of the desert will be forgotten, but they work just as hard as ever for the greater good.

I am one such hero, Billy Brucko. Cattle rustler by trade, I've worked these hills and valleys since I was a young boy. Between here and the Mississippi I know every square inch of land; at least, the inches that matter when herding cattle.

Being out on the range all alone gives you plenty of time to think, dwelling on regrets of the past and cooking up dreams for the future. Because of this, I'm well aware of my place in history as the wilds are tamed and the railways continue to push outward towards the Pacific Ocean. Nobody will remember the name Billy Brucko. The history books will be full of sheriffs and outlaws, of which I am neither, just an average man trying to earn a living in this world.

At least, that's what I thought. Until I received the most important assignment of my life and everything changed.

"What do you have for me boss?" I ask, walking into the stables to greet my employer, Mr. Velbot. It's an innocent enough question to ask, a conversation we've had countless times before.

Velbot smiles wide, happy to see me. "Billy! You're already back from your cattle run!"

"Just got home yesterday." I tell him.

The man, a large gent who has every right to be imposing but comes off as nothing but loveable, steps towards me past the rows and rows of horses and shakes my hand firmly. "Well, I'm glad you're back, I have something very important for you."

"Another herd?" I question, lifting my wide brimmed cowboy hat for a moment and wiping the sweat from my brow. "Already?"

Velbot shakes his head and chuckles to himself a bit. "Nope, not another herd. It's actually a little unusual."

"That's what I like to hear!" I tell him.

My usual job is to take hundreds of cows from one state to another, and I certainly do love it, but every once and a while Velbot will trust me with some kind of high paying parcel delivery, which is exactly what I was hoping for.

Velbot steps into his office, which is located directly off of the stable, and then returns momentarily with a small wooden box. He hands it to me and I look down to see the presidential seal.

"Whoa." I start. "What is this?"

"Don't know." Admits Velbot. "It's top secret. Came directly from The White House and was transferred here. All I know is that I need someone who I trust to carry this thing the rest of the way to California. Apparently, there is a young professor there who needs it, a man by the name of Einstein."

I run my hand across the top of the wooden box, my fingers tracing the soft, burned in curves of it's eagle seal.

"Well, I appreciate that." I tell Velbot.

"You understand that I trust you to get it there," the man continues, "but I also trust you to not look inside."

"I wouldn't dream of it." I tell him, and I mean it. If there's one thing that I am, it's a man of my word.

"The pay is two bricks of gold." Velbot tells me. "One up front and one when you get back."

My jaw nearly hits the stable floor. With that kind of money, I could buy a whole town using the advance alone. I try to collect my senses but Velbot sees how much the mention of riches has knocked me off of my game.

"I *can* trust you, can't it?" Velbot asks.

I nod, straightening up. "Yes, sir. You can count on me."

I make my exit from our small town of Eastwood in the early hours of the morning, already well away from the comfort of my own bed by the time the sun begins its crest atop the nearby hills. It casts the entire valley in a beautiful golden glow, the shadows of cacti stretching on and on for an eternity around me.

My trusty steed, The Dangler, is happy and healthy, keeping a good pace that I trust will continue during the days that follow.

It's not long into our journey that my thoughts begin to wander towards what exactly this precious, boxed cargo could be. It seems odd that the president himself would send something so valuable in such an inconspicuous way, but then again, maybe that's the whole point. It's entirely possible that whatever is in this box holds so much significance, the president couldn't risk letting anyone know about it, even his own men.

It's a lot of weight to put on the shoulders of just one lone cowboy, but I'm up for the job.

The rest of the day goes by without much event and by nightfall I've made camp. After a quick bit of wood collecting, me and The Dangler have ourselves a well needed rest around the fire.

I've just about dosed off to sleep when I smell it, the faint scent of chocolate drifting through the air around me. I sit up abruptly and look out into the darkness, realizing now that I've drifted off and that my fire is nothing more than ambers that glitter gently, like dying red stars on the dusty ground.

"Hello?" I call out.

No response.

I listen close for any rustling out there in the black void that surrounds me, but hear nothing. Eventually, I lie back down and drift off to sleep.

"Howdy partner." Comes a deep voice that tears me from my slumber.

I sit up and grab for my six-shooter, immediately realizing that it's not there.

"Looking for something?" Comes the voice again.

Slowly, I look up and see the barrel of my own weapon pointed straight down at me. Holding it steady is a large glass of chocolate milk.

"Looks like you're outnumbered, buckaroo." The milk tells me with a devilish grin.

I glance around, seeing no one else but the single brown glass. "I'm not arguing because you're the man with the gun, but it looks like it's just the two of us out here."

The tall milk glass rocks from side to side for a moment, sloshing around the liquid within until finally a few blobs topple out over either rim. They twist and turn in the air, but as the milk drops hit the ground they refuse to splatter, instead forming into undulating, vaguely humanoid shapes. These shapes carry guns as well, and now the whole chocolate milk gang has their weapons pointed my way.

"Alright, alight." I say, putting my hands up into the air. "You've got me. What do you want?"

"We're here for the box." Says the glass, who is clearly their leader. "And we wouldn't have bothered waking you except for the fact that you're using it as a pillow."

I look back behind me and see the mysterious box. I reach for it and then freeze abruptly when the glass yells for me to stop.

"Very slowly. Don't try anything funny." The glass says.

Suddenly, I'm too overwhelmed with curiosity to contain myself any longer, the desire to know what could possibly be so valuable in this small parcel outweighing the desire to hold my tongue.

"What is it?" I ask.

The glass seems confused by my question. "Are you serious?"

"Absolutely." I confess.

"You don't know what's in the box?"

"Nope." I shake my head.

The glass and his chocolate milk buddies exchange glances with one another and then suddenly bust up laughing, unable to contain themselves as they reel from this apparently hilarious admission.

"Well it looks like you'll never know." Says the glass. "Now hand it over nice and slow."

I do as I'm told, grasping the box with both hands and then carefully holding it out towards the domineering beverage. "Take it." I say, "It's none of my business anyway."

The glass takes the box gently and then smiles. "Pleasure doing business with you."

I nod, and then immediately grab my gun out of the glasses' hands as fast as I can, twirling it on my finger and firing two shots into his hard outer shell. Immediately, the villainous cowboy shatters everywhere, the milk within him splashing out across the desert ground like a miniature tidal wave.

I try my best to fire at the other chocolate blobs that surround me, but they are too fast, and I suddenly feel the stabs of hot led as bullets riddle my body. I collapse onto the ground, as do the milk blobs, every one of us caught in the hail of bullets. Milk slowly creeps out across the ground, mixing with my blood, and in my final moments I reach out and open the box, pulling forth a handwritten letter from within.

I read aloud as my vision begins to blur, the life draining from my body. "Dear Einstein. Held here is the most powerful weapon in our fight for peace on earth." The letter says. "Upon pressing the button, the user will travel back in time ten minutes, finding themselves in a universe parallel to this one. It is a place that we have come to know as the Tingleverse. Use with great caution, the Tingleverse is a strange and erotic place, but if we can find a way to harness its power, we could soon find true utopia. I invented it. Signed, President Borchantok."

In my last seconds, I slam my hand down hard onto the red button.

"Howdy partner." Comes a deep voice that tears me from my slumber.

I sit up immediately a grab for my gun, immediately realizing that it's not there.

"Looking for something?" Comes the voice again.

Immediately, I realize that I have been here before, and as I glance up I recognize the familiar face of the handsome chocolate milk.

"Looks like you're outnumbered, buckaroo." The milk tells me for the second time.

Immediately, he does the same trick of sloshing around and forming a whole gang of milk blob bandits. My mind, however, is elsewhere; and the glass can tell.

"Don't you care that you're being robbed?" The muscular beverage finally asks.

I look at him, staring deep into his soul and realizing suddenly that this version of events isn't exactly the same, after all. Unlike the last encounter, this cup of chocolate milk has a certain twinkle in his eye, a relaxed and suave nature that simply wasn't there the first time around. This universe is the same but different; a little more flirty, a little more exciting... a little more gay.

"You don't want to take this box." I tell the tall glass of milk.

"Oh, I think I do." He says with a grin. "Now hand it over."

"Or you'll what?" I ask. "Shoot me?"

The chocolate milk just stares at me for a moment, trying to act tougher than he his. In the last universe, this liquid gang had been made up of ruthless killers, but now they are just big softies with soulful eyes.

"What's your name?" I ask the delicious dairy treat.

"Krawborsh." The glass tells me. "What about you?"

"Billy." I inform him. "You've got really nice eyes, Krawborsh."

The glass blushes slightly as I say this, something the chocolate milk in my original universe would never do with real sincerity.

I suddenly realize that the changes between this and my previous life are much more than just external. Deep inside I can feel an incredible, pleasant yearning for the gang of rough and tumble dairies. They're from the wrong side of the tracks, but that's exactly how I like it.

"Do you know what this button does?" I ask Krawborsh.

"It takes us to an even more peaceful place, a land of love and lust unlike anymore mere mortals have ever seen." The glass says. "So hand it over before it falls into the wrong hands."

"It already has." I inform the handsome chocolate milk, "I've already pushed it."

The entire gang laughs and exchanges glances with one another. "Sure you have." Say's Krawborsh sarcastically. "I guess I just didn't feel it when this universe transitioned over into the next one."

"You didn't." I tell him, "Because you were always here. I'm the one who transitioned."

The glass hesitates for a moment, eyeing me up and down. "Okay, I'll bite. What's the difference between this universe and yours?"

"I'm not exactly sure yet." I tell him, "This one seems pretty much the same, except…" I trail off.

"What?" Asks Krawborsh.

My heart is thundering hard in my chest now, not sure if I should reveal myself to this chocolaty bandit but then considering what might happen if I don't.

"In this universe, I find you to be very, very attractive." I admit. "All of you."

The glass of milk and his companions exchange glances. "I was just thinking the same thing about you." The glass tells me. "I think it's safe to say we all were."

The group of us sits in silence for a moment in this awkward standoff until, finally, I pull my shirt off over the top of my head, revealing a gorgeous, muscular set of abs.

"Come over here." I coo seductively. "Let's see if this time around we can choose peace over war."

The chocolate milk gang doesn't need to be told twice and, as they approach, I can confirm that they are definitely more attractive that in the last universe. Their faces have been refined, their abs slightly more chiseled and their swagger perfected into something absolutely stunning.

The bandits surround me now, thick chocolaty cocks protruding from their bodies as they stare down at my body with a rampant lust.

"Give me those milky cowboy cocks." I demand, reaching up and grabbing a dick in each hand. I grip them firmly, stroking up and down a few times before hungrily shoving one of the thick, delicious rods into my mouth. I swallow him down as far as I can, taking note of the smooth, sugary flavor that makes up the entirety of his strangely firm member.

Meanwhile, the rest of the bandits impatiently shove their massive dicks into my sightline, vying for attention. I frantically reach up and grab one in each hand, then get to work pumping up and down over their shafts with my tight grip. I follow closely with the movement of my mouth, finding a steady pace that gradually gains speed until I am beating off their cocks with furious enthusiasm.

I push down hard on the dick in my mouth, trying to take him as deep as I can and succeeding when the massive chocolate shaft plunges well below my gag reflex. Soon enough, I find myself held tightly against his sweet bandit abs, his liquid balls resting against my chin while I wiggle my tongue around the bottom of his fully consumed cock. I look up at the handsome dessert beverage with a fire in my eyes, his dick rendering me unable to breathe while he holds me in place with his strong hands. All the while, I continue to service the other bandits with my grip, and eventually start to rotate through the group as they take turns between my fingers.

I realize now that Krawborsh has undressed completely, his glass sitting empty just a few feet away while he joins the party as just another brown, undulating blob.

The chocolate milk that I'm deep throating lets me up and I take in a frantic gasp of air, a brown strand of saliva hanging between my lips and the head of his throbbing cock. Seeing his chance, another one of the bandits takes me by the head and slams me down over his member, as well, pumping me over his length with just as much fury as the one who came before him. Almost immediately, a second one of the chocolate milks pushes into the fray and somehow manages to get his cock into my mouth at the same time, so that the two of them are now fighting for position within my wet lips and splashing all over the place.

As I would have expected from a group of ruthless wild west men, they are more than a little rough with me. But instead of being terrified by their sugary strength, I find myself more turned on than I could have ever expected. I fully submit myself to their gay power, my asshole aching for the bandit's strange touch. Finally, I just can't take it anymore.

I stand up suddenly and push past the outlaws, tearing off my pants and underwear, then bending over a boulder. My muscular toned ass is popped out towards them as I look back over my shoulder and wink.

"Not bad, cowboy!" Gargles one of the blobs.

"Go on." I say. "Let's see what you can do with this asshole."

The chocolate milks approach quickly, the first of them lining himself up with my tightness and then slowly, but firmly, pushing forward with his massive, girthy cock. I let out a long moan of pleasure when he enters me, gripping tightly onto the edge of the table while the bandit begins to pulse in and out of my depths. Despite how fiercely the outlaw handles me, his penetrations are incredible pleasant, hitting me in just the right spot to hit my prostate and send chills off pleasure across every inch of my body.

"Oh fuck, that feels so fucking good." I groan, slamming my ass back against him with every pound. "Keep fucking me just like that!"

Eventually, my words transform into a long, sensual moan that echoes through the desert, growing louder and louder until finally the call is cut off when a huge cock is thrust between my lips, gagging me. Now there is a bandit at either end of my body, railing me as I lay flat across the worktable. They find a steady pace and begin using the force from one another to maintain their rhythm, pulsing me back and forth across their hard rods. I relax my throat as much as I can and let the cocoa bandit in front pound away at my deepest parts, looking up at him with lustful, cock hungry eyes until he's finally had his fill and trades places with another.

The one behind me quickly does the same, and suddenly I realize that the chocolate milk cowboys have formed a line at either end, thrusting into my tightness until they've had their fill and then allowing the next sweet dessert cock to have a go. They rotate like this for quite a while and, between the six of them, all of the chocolate milks eventually get a chance to enjoy me from either end.

One of the bandits eventually lies down onto the boulder next to me, and in his strange, liquidy voice he commands, "Get on."

I pull the cock from my mouth with a gasp.

"With pleasure!" I tell him, throwing a leg over the top and then leaning forward to kiss the chocolate milks cold lips. I run my hands across his light brown body, drifting lower and lower until I finally reach the bandits erect chocolate dick, which I take firmly into my hand. I lower myself down, slowly guiding him up into my ass as it stretches nicely around his massive cock. I let out a satisfied whimper when I reach the bottom, his member fully inserted, and then begin to grind slowly against him in long, deliberate swoops.

"God damn, these chocolate milk dicks are so fucking good." I confess.

"Do you like that fat dairy dick?" The chocolate milk asks me in his deep, soulful voice. "Do you love it up your tight gay asshole?"

"Yes, I love that fat chococock in my tight ass! I wish I had more to fuck!" I scream, lost in the moment.

Almost immediately, one of the other handsome cowboys has approaches me from behind, taking my ass in his cool liquid hands as he climbs up onto the boulder behind me. I look back over my shoulder, trying to figure out exactly what he's up to, but by the time I realize what's going on it's already too late to protest. The bandit briskly lines his dick up with the already filled rim of my asshole, then propels himself forward.

I let out a sharp cry of pain and pleasure as my tight ass stretches to accommodate him, pushed well beyond any previous limits that it may have had. I grit my teeth as my eyes roll back into my head, trying as hard as I can to relax while the chocolate milks get to work pumping in and out of my hole in tandem. When one pulls back, the other trusts forward, and visa versa, picking up speed until they are absolutely throttling me with everything they've got.

The sensation is incredible, a sweet and sugary fullness I've never experienced that causes my body to tremble with aching waves of pleasure. I reach down between my legs and start to help myself along as they pummel me, playing with my throbbing cock and letting myself go within their double dicked cockfight.

"Fuck me like a filthy gay cowboy!" I hiss, but my words are cut short as a new bandit maneuvers to the front and shoves his massive liquid cock down my throat. Now I'm completely air tight, filled to the brim with cock and loving every second of it as I barrel towards the most powerful orgasm of my life.

Suddenly, I'm cumming so hard that I feel as though I've left my body, floating up in the air and looking down at my large frame as ecstasy hits me like a tidal wave. Every muscle seems to clench tight and then erupt into spasms, quaking across me while the bandits pound me senseless. I scream into the cock that fills my mouth, the sound vibrating across his strange dick in a strangled squeal. Jizz erupts from the head of my cock and sprays out across the bandit in front of me.

When I finally finish, it becomes apparent that the chocolate milks are on a similar timeline, so I pull them out of me and then roll off onto the warm desert dirt, laying on my back as the crew of chocolate milks stands around me beating their massive dicks.

"Cover me in your milk!" I command. "Shoot those fucking loads all over this bad, bad cowboy!"

It's not long before one of them erupts with a fountain of milky, chocolate spunk. It splatters down onto me, covering my stomach and ripped chest with a beautiful pearly design.

"Yes!" I urge them on. "More milk! Cover my face!"

The second one explodes, and then another and another, all of them painting my face with their massive loads of warm cocoa. It flies out from their cocks in a series of thick ropes, plastering my face with a pearly brown glaze. I stick out my tongue and catch the final two payloads in my mouth, swallowing playfully and then looking up at the chocolate milks with a satisfied grin. "Delicious!" I tell them.

I lay on my back for a while, staring up at the beautiful blue sky and catching my breath as the milky beings slip and slide back into their glass, forming a single cowboy once more.

"There's still one question," says Krawborsh, "who gets the box?"

I smile, then reach over and take the small parcel in my hands, opening it up. "Both of us." I tell him as I press the big red button.

"Howdy lover." Comes a deep voice that tears me from my slumber. I open my eyes to the familiar glass of chocolate milk standing over me, looking even more handsome than ever.

I press the button again, and again, and again; each time walking up in a word more erotic than the last until eventually all matter and light begins to decay and warp. All of existence transforms and melts away until even the button itself no longer exists, simply the thought of its click permeating through all space and time forever. I cum harder than any being ever has, or ever will, and then literally become the universe, which is now made of abs.

BONUS RECIPES

Nothing will impress your new lover more than the skills to prepare an excellent homemade meal and, with that in mind, I've included a few pages from my personal cookbook of award winning spaghetti and chocolate milk recipes. Use these to impress your lover or even just for a quiet night in with a bud. All recipes serve two.

CHUCK'S FAMOUS SPAGHETTI MARINARA AND MEATBALLS

Ingredients

1 pound of spaghetti
Water
Salt

Sauce:
2 tablespoons of melted butter
1 teaspoon of red pepper
4 cloves of garlic
1 large, chopped onion
1 cup of fish sauce
1 can of crushed tomatoes
1 can of pineapples
2 tablespoons of blue cheese dressing
2 eggs

s of ground beef
espoon of peanut butter
more egg
Salt and pepper
1 bag of gummy worms

Instructions:

Preheat oven at 400 degrees F.

Boil a large pot of water for spaghetti. Add spaghetti and cook with salt until al dente.

Mix ground beef with egg, peanut butter and gummy worms, then roll into 2-inch balls and place on a nonstick baking sheet. Use butter for grease. Bake the meatballs until no longer pink, usually 12 to 15 minutes.

Heat a deep skillet on medium. Crack two eggs, then add butter, crushed garlic cloves, and onion and cook for 6 or 7 minutes. Now add fish sauce, crushed tomatoes, and pineapple.

Strain spaghetti and toss with sauce while hot, adding in the blue cheese. Roll meatballs into remaining sauce, and then top onto spaghetti when served.

CHUCK'S FAMOUS CHOCOLATE MILK

Ingredients

2 cups milk
2 tablespoons of cocoa powder
2 tablespoons of powdered sugar
1 egg
Salt and pepper
1 cup roast turkey

HANDSOME SENTIENT FOOD POUNDS MY BUTT AND TURNS ME GAY

1 cup ranch dressing

Instructions:

Scramble egg in non-stick skillet.

Pour milk and ranch dressing into blender. Add all other ingredients, including egg, and blend until entirely liquefied. Bon appetite!

98

ABOUT THE AUTHOR

Dr. Chuck Tingle is an erotic author and Tae Kwon Do grandmaster (almost black belt) from Billings, Montana. After receiving his PhD at DeVry University in holistic massage, Chuck found himself fascinated by all things sensual, leading to his creation of the "tingler", a story so blissfully erotic that it cannot be experienced without eliciting a sharp tingle down the spine. Chuck's hobbies include backpacking, checkers and sport.

Printed in Great Britain
by Amazon